The Stranger in the Lifeboat

The Stranger
in the Lifeboat

Mitch Albom

SPHERE

SPHERE

First published in the United States in 2021 by HarperCollins
First published in Great Britain in 2021 by Sphere

1 3 5 7 9 10 8 6 4 2

A CIP catalogue record for this book is available from the British Library.

Hardback ISBN 978-0-7515-8453-0

Printed and bound in the UK by Clays Ltd, Elcograf S.p.A.
Designed by Leah Carlson-Stanisic

Papers used by Sphere are from well-managed forests
and other responsible sources.

Sphere
An imprint of
Little, Brown Book Group
Carmelite House
50 Victoria Embankment
London EC4Y 0DZ

An Hachette UK Company
www.hachette.co.uk

www.littlebrown.co.uk

To Janine, Trisha, and Connie, who show me, every day, the stunning power of belief

The Stranger in the Lifeboat

One

Sea

~~~~~~

When we pulled him from the water, he didn't have a scratch on him. That's the first thing I noticed. The rest of us were all gashes and bruises, but he was unmarked, with smooth almond skin and thick dark hair matted by seawater. He was bare-chested, not particularly muscular, maybe twenty years old, and his eyes were pale blue, the color you imagine the ocean to be when you dream of a tropical vacation—not the endless gray waves that surround this crowded lifeboat, waiting for us like an open grave.

Forgive me for such despair, my love. It's been three days since the *Galaxy* sank. No one has come looking for us. I try to stay positive, to believe rescue is near. But we are short on food and water. Sharks have been spotted. I see surrender in the eyes of many on board. The words *We're going to die* have been uttered too many times.

If that is to be, if this is indeed my end, then I am writing to you in the pages of this notebook, Annabelle, in hopes you might somehow read them after I am gone. I need to tell you something, and I need to tell the world as well.

I could begin with why I was on the *Galaxy* that night, or Dobby's plan, or my deep sense of guilt at the yacht exploding, even though I cannot be sure of what happened. But for now, the story must begin with this morning, when we pulled the young stranger from the sea. He wore no life jacket, nor was he holding on to anything when we spotted him bobbing in the waves. We let him catch his breath, and from our various perches in the boat, we introduced ourselves.

Lambert, the boss, spoke first, saying, "Jason Lambert, I owned the *Galaxy*." Then came Nevin, the tall Brit, who apologized that he could not rise for a proper welcome, having gashed his leg trying to escape the sinking vessel. Geri just nodded and balled up the line she had used to tug the man in. Yannis offered a weak handshake. Nina mumbled "Hi." Mrs. Laghari, the woman from India, said nothing; she didn't seem to trust the newcomer. Jean Philippe, the Haitian cook, smiled and said, "Welcome, brother," but kept a palm on the shoulder of his sleeping wife, Bernadette, who is wounded from the explosion, badly wounded, I believe. The little girl we call Alice, who hasn't spoken since we found her clinging to a deck chair in the ocean, remained silent.

I went last. "Benji," I said. "My name is Benji." For some reason my voice caught in my throat.

We waited for the stranger to respond, but he just looked at us, doe-eyed. Lambert said, "He's probably in shock." Nevin yelled, "HOW LONG WERE YOU IN THE WATER?" perhaps thinking a raised voice would snap him to his senses. When he didn't answer, Nina touched his shoulder and said, "Well, thank the Lord we found you."

Which is when the man finally spoke.

"I *am* the Lord," he whispered.

Land

The inspector put out his cigarette. His chair creaked. It was already hot on this Montserrat morning, and his starched white shirt stuck to his sweaty back. His temples were throbbing from a hangover headache. He gazed at the thin, bearded man who'd been waiting for him when he arrived at the police station.

"Let's start again," the inspector said.

It was Sunday. He had been in bed when the call came. *A man is here. He says he found a raft from that American yacht that blew up.* The inspector mumbled a curse. His wife, Patrice, groaned and rolled over on her pillow.

"What time did you get home last night?" she mumbled.

"Late."

"How late?"

He dressed without answering her, made instant coffee, poured it into a Styrofoam cup, and kicked the door frame as he left the house, banging his big toe. It still hurt.

"My name is Jarty LeFleur," he said now, sizing up the man across the desk. "I am the chief inspector for the island. And your name is . . ."

"Rom, Inspector."

"Do you have a last name, Rom?"

"Yes, Inspector."

LeFleur sighed. "What is it?"

"Rosh, Inspector."

LeFleur wrote it down, then lit another cigarette. He rubbed his head. He needed aspirin.

"So you found a raft, Rom?"

"Yes, Inspector."

"Where?"

"Marguerita Bay."

"When?"

"Yesterday."

LeFleur looked up to see the man staring at a desk photo of LeFleur and his wife swinging their young daughter over a beach towel.

"Is that your family?" Rom asked.

"Don't look at that," LeFleur snapped. "Look at me. This raft. How did you know it was from the *Galaxy*?"

"It's written on the inside."

"And you just found it, washed up on the beach?"

"Yes, Inspector."

"Nobody with it?"

"No, Inspector."

LeFleur was sweating. He moved the desk fan closer. The story was plausible. All kinds of things washed up on the north shore. Suitcases, parachutes, drugs, fish-aggregating contraptions that swept into the currents and floated across the North Atlantic.

Nothing was too strange to roll in with the tide. But a raft from the *Galaxy*? That would be a major event. The huge luxury yacht had sunk last year, fifty miles from Cape Verde off the West African coast. It made news around the world, mostly because of all the rich and famous people who'd been on board. None of them were found.

LeFleur rocked back and forth. *That raft didn't inflate itself.* Maybe the authorities were wrong. Maybe someone had survived the *Galaxy* tragedy, at least briefly.

"OK, Rom," he said, snuffing out his cigarette. "Let's go take a look."

Sea

~~~~~~

"I *am* the Lord."

What do you say to that, my love? Maybe under normal conditions you laugh or make a wisecrack. *You're the Lord? Buy the drinks.* But alone in the middle of this ocean, thirsty and desperate, well, it unnerved me, to be honest.

"What did he just say?" Nina whispered.

"He said he was the *Lord*," Lambert scoffed.

"You got a first name, Lord?" Yannis asked.

"I have many names," the stranger said. His voice was calm but husky, almost hoarse.

"And you've been swimming for three days?" Mrs. Laghari interjected. "That's impossible."

"She's right," Geri said. "The water temperature is sixty-seven degrees. You can't live in that for three days."

Geri is the most experienced sea person among us. She was an Olympic swimmer when she was younger and has that take-charge tone—confident, curt, intolerant of stupid questions—that makes people pay heed.

"DID YOU FLOAT IN SOMETHING?" Nevin yelled.

"For Christ's sake, Nevin," Yannis said, "he's not deaf."

The stranger looked at Yannis when he said "for Christ's sake," and Yannis closed his mouth, as if trying to suck the words back in.

"What's your real story, mister?" Lambert said.

"I am here," the stranger said.

"*Why* are you here?" Nina asked.

"Haven't you been calling me?"

We glanced at one another. We are a pathetic-looking lot, faces blistered by the sun, clothes crusted by salt water. We can't fully stand up without falling into someone, and the floor smells of rubber, glue, and vomit from our retching. It is true, most of us, at some point, thrashing in the waves that first night or staring at the empty horizon in the days that followed, have cried out for divine intervention. *Please, Lord! . . . Help us, God!* Is that what this new man meant? *Haven't you been calling me?* As you know, Annabelle, I have struggled with faith much of my life. I was a dutiful altar boy, like many Irish kids, but the church and I parted company years ago. What happened with my mother. What happened with you. Too much disappointment. Not enough comfort.

Still, I never considered what I would do if I called for the Lord and He actually appeared before me.

"Is there any water you can share?" the man asked.

"God is thirsty?" Lambert said, laughing. "Great. Anything else?"

"Perhaps something to eat?"

"This is foolish," Mrs. Laghari grumbled. "He's obviously playing games."

"No!" Nina yelled abruptly, her face contorting like a denied child. "Let him talk." She spun toward the man. "Are you here to save us?"

His voice softened. "I can only do that," he said, "when everyone here believes I am who I say I am."

No one moved. You could hear the smack of the sea against the boat's sides. Finally, Geri, who is too practical for talk like this, surveyed the group like an annoyed schoolteacher.

"Well, buddy," she said, "you let us know when that happens. Until then, we better adjust our food rations."

News

REPORTER: *This is Valerie Cortez, aboard the* Galaxy, *the spectacular yacht owned by Jason Lambert. The billionaire businessman has assembled some of the biggest names in the world for a weeklong adventure, and he's here with us now. Hello, Jason.*

LAMBERT: *Welcome, Valerie.*

REPORTER: *You've called this extravaganza "the Grand Idea." Why?*

LAMBERT: *Because everyone on this ship has done something grand, something to shape their industry, their country, maybe even the planet. We have technology leaders, business leaders, political leaders, entertainment leaders. They're big-idea people.*

REPORTER: *Movers and shakers, like yourself.*

LAMBERT: *Well. Ha. I don't know about that.*

REPORTER: *And you brought them together for what reason?*

LAMBERT: *Valerie, it's a $200 million yacht. I think a good time is possible!*

REPORTER: *Obviously!*

LAMBERT: *No. Seriously. Idea people need to be around other idea people. They spur each other to change the world.*

REPORTER: *So this is like the World Economic Forum in Davos, Switzerland?*

LAMBERT: *Right. But a more fun version—on water.*

REPORTER: *And you hope many grand ideas come out of this trip?*

LAMBERT: *That, and some quality hangovers.*

REPORTER: *Hangovers, did you say?*

LAMBERT: *What's life without a party, Valerie? Am I right?*

Sea

~~~~~~

Lambert throws up. He is on his knees, heaving over the side. His fat midsection protrudes from his T-shirt, and he is hairy at the navel. Some of the vomit blows back in his face, and he groans.

It is evening. The sea is choppy. Others have been sick as well. The winds are fierce. Maybe it will rain. We've had no rain since the *Galaxy* sank.

Looking back, we were still hopeful that first morning— shocked at what happened, but grateful to be alive. The ten of us huddled inside the lifeboat. We spoke about rescue planes. We scanned the horizon.

"Who here has children?" Mrs. Laghari suddenly asked, as if starting a car game. "I myself have two. Grown now."

"Three," Nevin offered.

"Five," Lambert said. "Got you beat."

"But how many wives?" Nevin poked.

"That wasn't the question," Lambert said.

"I've been too busy," Yannis said.

"Not yet for me," Nina said.

"Have you got a husband?" Mrs. Laghari asked.

"Do I need one?"

Mrs. Laghari laughed. "Well, I did! Anyhow, you won't have any problem in that department."

"We have four sons," Jean Philippe announced. He rested a hand on his sleeping wife's shoulder. "Bernadette and I. Four good boys." He turned to me. "And you, Benji?"

"No kids, Jean Philippe."

"Do you have a wife?"

I hesitated.

"Yes."

"Well, then, you can start when we get home!"

He flashed a broad smile, and the group laughed a little. But as the day went on, the waves grew bumpier and we all got seasick. By evening, the mood had changed. It felt as if we'd been out here a week. I remember seeing little Alice sleeping in Nina's lap, and Nina's face streaked with tears. Mrs. Laghari grabbed her hand as Nina whimpered, "What if they can't *find* us?"

What if they can't? Without a compass, Geri has been trying to chart our course by the stars. She thinks we are heading southwest, away from Cape Verde and farther into the wide, empty Atlantic. That is not good.

Meanwhile, to avoid direct sunlight, we spend hours tucked under a stretched canopy that covers more than half of the boat. We must sit inches from one another, stripped down, sweaty, foul-smelling. It's a far cry from the *Galaxy*, even if some of us were guests on that luxury vessel and some of us workers. Here we are all the same. Half-naked and scared.

The Grand Idea—the voyage that brought us all together—was Lambert's brainchild. He told invitees they were there to change the world. I never believed that. The yacht's size. Its multiple decks. The swimming pool, gym, the ballroom. That's what he wanted them to remember.

As for workers like Nina, Bernadette, Jean Philippe, and me? We were only there to serve. I have labored under Jason Lambert for five months now, and I have never felt so invisible. Staff on the *Galaxy* are forbidden to make eye contact with guests, nor can we eat in their presence. Meanwhile, Lambert does what he wants, barreling into the kitchen, using his fingers to pick at the food, stuffing his face as the workers lower their heads. Everything about him screams gluttony, from his flashy rings to his obese midsection. I can see why Dobby wanted him dead.

I turn away from Lambert's puking and study the new arrival, who is sleeping outside the canopy with his mouth
slightly open. He is not particularly striking for a man
who claims to be the Almighty. His eyebrows are thick,
his cheeks are flabby, he has a wide chin and small ears,
partly covered by that dark nest of hair. I admit I felt a chill
when he said those things yesterday: *I am here . . . Have
you not been calling me?* But later, when Geri handed out
packets of peanut butter crackers, he ripped open the plastic and devoured the contents so quickly, I thought he'd
choke. I doubt God would ever get that hungry. Certainly
not for peanut butter crackers.

Still, for the moment, he has distracted us. Earlier, as he
slept, we gathered to whisper our theories.

"Do you think he's delirious?"

"Of course! He probably banged his head."

"There's no way he survived three days treading water."

"What's the longest a man can do that?"

"I read about a guy who lasted twenty-eight hours."

"Still not three days."

"He honestly thinks he's *God*?"

"He had no life jacket!"

"Maybe he came from another boat."

"If there were another boat, we would have seen it."

Finally, Nina spoke up. She was the *Galaxy*'s hairstylist,
born in Ethiopia. With her high cheekbones and flowing

dark locks, she retains a certain elegance even here in the middle of the sea. "Has anyone considered the least likely explanation?" she asked.

"Which is?" Yannis said.

"That he's telling the truth? That he's come in our hour of need?"

Eyes darted from one to the next. Then Lambert started laughing, a deep, dismissive cackle. "Oh, yes! That's how we all picture God. Floating like seaweed until you pull him into your boat. Come on. Did you look at him? He's like some island kid who fell off his surfboard."

We shifted our legs. No one said much after that. I looked up at the pale white moon, which hung large in the sky. Do some of us think it possible? That this strange new arrival is actually the Lord incarnate?

I can only speak for myself.

No, I do not.

Land

LeFleur drove the man called Rom to the north shore of the island. He tried to make conversation, but Rom answered with polite deflections: "Yes, Inspector" and "No, Inspector." LeFleur eyed the glove compartment, where he kept a small flask of whisky.

"You live up by St. John's?" LeFleur tried.

Rom half nodded.

"Where do you go liming?"

Rom looked at him blankly.

"Liming? Chilling? Hanging out?"

No response. They drove past a rum shop and a boarded-up disco/café, with turquoise shutters hanging loosely off their hinges.

"What about surfing? You do any surfing? Bransby Point? Trants Bay?"

"I don't care much for the water."

"Come on, man," LeFleur laughed. "You're on an island!"

Rom looked straight ahead. The inspector gave up. He reached for another cigarette. Through his rolled-down window, he glanced back at the mountains.

Twenty-four years before, Montserrat's volcano, Soufrière Hills, erupted after centuries of silence, covering the entire southern part of the island in mud and ash. The capital was destroyed. Lava smothered the airport. Just like that, the nation's economy evaporated in dark smoke. Two-thirds of the population fled Montserrat within a year, mostly to England, where they were given emergency citizen status. Even now, the island's southern half remains uninhabited, an ash-covered "exclusion zone" of abandoned towns and villas.

LeFleur glanced at his passenger, who was tapping annoyingly on the door handle. He thought about calling Patrice, apologizing for this morning, leaving so abruptly. Instead he reached across Rom's chest, mumbled "Excuse me," and popped open the glove compartment, removing the whisky flask.

"You want some?" he asked.

"No, thank you, Inspector."

"Don't drink?"

"Not anymore."

"How come?"

"I drank to forget things."

"And?"

"I kept remembering them."

LeFleur paused, then took a swig. They drove in silence the rest of the way.

Sea

~~~~~~

Dear Annabelle—

The "Lord" has not saved us. He has worked no magic. He's done little and said even less. He will apparently be just another mouth to feed and another body to make room for.

The wind and waves kicked back up today, so we all squeezed for shelter under the canopy. This puts us knee to knee, elbow to elbow. I sat with Mrs. Laghari on one side and the new man on another. At times I brushed against his bare skin. It felt no different than my own.

"Come on, 'Lord,' tell us the truth," Lambert said, pointing at the new man. "How did you get on my boat?"

"I was never on your boat," he replied.

"Then how did you fall into the ocean?" Geri asked.

"I did not fall."

"What were you doing in the water?"

"Coming to you."

We looked at one another.

"Let me get this straight," Yannis said. "God decided to drop from the sky, swim to this raft, and start talking to us?"

"I talk to you all the time," he said. "I came here to listen."

"Listen to what?" I said.

"Enough!" Lambert broke in. "If you know so much, tell me what happened to my *damn yacht*!"

The man smiled. "Why are you angry about that?"

"I lost my boat!"

"You are in another."

"It's not the same!"

"True," the man said. "This one is still afloat."

Yannis chuckled. Lambert glared at him.

"What?" Yannis said. "It's funny."

Mrs. Laghari exhaled impatiently. "May we stop with this nonsense? Where are the planes? The ones that rescue us? Tell us that, and I will pray to you right now."

We waited for a reply. But the man just sat there, shirtless and grinning. The mood shifted. Mrs. Laghari had reminded us that, despite this newcomer's odd distraction, we remain hopelessly lost.

"Nobody's praying to him," Lambert grumbled.

News

REPORTER: *This is Valerie Cortez, aboard the* Galaxy *yacht, owned by billionaire investor Jason Lambert. As you can see, it's raining, so I'm tucked in here. But the exorbitant fun continues on this fifth and final night of the Grand Idea.*

ANCHOR: *What took place today, Valerie?*

REPORTER: *Today the attendees were treated to discussion groups led by a former US president, the designer of the world's first electric car, and the founders of the three biggest computer search engines in the world, the first time they were ever on the same stage together.*

ANCHOR: *What's that music in the background?*

REPORTER: *Well, Jim, I think I mentioned that this yacht has a helicopter landing pad. They've been bringing people back and forth all week. Earlier today, the popular rock band Fashion X was flown in to perform. You can hear them in the ballroom behind me. I think that's their big hit, "Coming Down."*

ANCHOR: *Wow. That's impressive.*

REPORTER: *It is. And once they are finished, there's—*

(Loud noise. The image shakes.)

ANCHOR: *Valerie, what was that?*
REPORTER: *I don't know! Hold on—*

(Another loud noise. She falls.)

REPORTER: *Oh my god! . . . Does anybody know what that—*
ANCHOR: *Valerie?*
REPORTER: *Something just hit . . .* (static) *. . . sounded . . .* (static) *. . . see where . . .*

(Another loud noise, then the picture is lost.)

ANCHOR: *Valerie? Valerie, can you still hear us? . . . Valerie? . . . We seem to have lost the connection. There was a loud noise, several, as you heard. We don't want to speculate. But for the moment, we are unable to . . . Hello? . . . Valerie? . . . Are you there? . . .*

Land

When his jeep reached the lookout point, LeFleur killed the engine. He had requested the area be marked off by the local authorities, and was relieved to see yellow tape by the walking path.

"All right," LeFleur said to Rom. "Let's see what you found."

They stepped over the tape and started down the path. Marguerita Bay was a stretch of rocky green hills that dropped off in craggy white walls, framing the shore and the narrow, sandy beach. There were several ways to get down, but not in a car. You went by foot.

As they reached the flat ground and approached the discovery site, Rom slowed his pace, leaving LeFleur to draw near on his own. He felt the sand give way to his work shoes. A few more steps around a low rock formation and . . .

There it was: a large, half-inflated, dirty orange raft, drying in the midday sun.

LeFleur felt a shiver. Wreckage of any vessel—ships, boats, rafts, yachts—meant another losing battle between man and sea. There were stories in their remains. Ghost stories. LeFleur had enough of those in his life already.

He leaned in to examine the raft's edges. Gashes had deflated the lower tubing. *Sharks could have done that.* The canopy had been ripped away, leaving only frayed pieces where it once attached to the frame. The faded words CAPACITY 15 PERSONS were etched on the orange skin. The inner floor was wide, maybe fourteen feet by sixteen feet. Sand and seaweed filled it now. Tiny crabs moved about the tangle.

LeFleur followed one crab as it moved past the etched words PROPERTY OF THE GALAXY and up to what appeared to be a sealed pouch along the front edge. A small lump was pushing the pouch outward. He touched the raft skin then pulled his hand back.

There was something inside.

LeFleur felt his pulse quicken. He knew the protocol: *owners of a vessel are to be notified before any lifeboat contents are disturbed.* But that could take a long time. And hadn't the owner died in the explosion? Hadn't everyone died?

He looked back at Rom, who stood a good forty feet away, staring at the clouds. What the hell, LeFleur thought, his Sunday was already ruined.

He opened the flap and pulled the contents out a few inches. He blinked twice to make sure he was seeing correctly. There, sealed inside a plastic bag, were the remains of a notebook.

Sea

~~~~~~

It is just after noon now. Our fourth day in this lifeboat. We have witnessed something highly unusual, Annabelle. It concerns the new arrival who claims to be the Lord. Perhaps I was wrong. There may be more to him than meets the eye.

Earlier this morning, Yannis was leaning on the raft's edge, singing a Greek song. (He's from Greece, an ambassador, I believe, even though he's quite young.) Geri was doing her navigation charts. Mrs. Laghari was rubbing her temples, trying to relieve her constant headaches. Alice, the little girl, was sitting with her arms wrapped around her knees. She was staring at the new man, as she has done much of the time since his arrival.

Suddenly he rose and moved across the raft to Jean Philippe, who was praying over his wife, Bernadette. Both are Haitian. Good people. Upbeat. I met them that first morning in Cape Verde, when the crew boarded the *Galaxy* to await the guests. They told me they'd been cooking on big boats for years.

"We make the food too good, Benji!" Bernadette said, patting her belly. "We get fat!"

"Why did you leave Haiti?" I asked.

"Oh, hard life there, Benji, hard life," she said.

"And you?" Jean Philippe asked me. "From where did you come?"

"Ireland, then America," I said.

"Why did you leave?" Bernadette said.

"Oh, hard life there, Bernadette, hard life."

We all laughed. Bernadette was often laughing. Her eyes made you feel welcome, and she would nod her head like a bobbing doll if you said something she agreed with. "Oh, *cherie*!" she'd intone. "You speak true!" But now she was unresponsive. She'd been badly injured escaping the yacht Friday night. Jean Philippe said she fell on the deck when the ship listed, and a large table crashed into her head and shoulders. She's been slipping in and out of consciousness for the last twenty-four hours.

Were we at home, she'd be in a hospital for sure. But out here, adrift, you realize how often we take our placement on this Earth for granted.

The new man leaned over Bernadette. Jean Philippe watched, his eyes widening.

"Are you truly the Lord?"

"Do you believe I am?"

"Prove it. Let me speak to my wife again."

I glanced at Yannis, who raised his eyebrows. How quickly we trust someone when the life of a loved one is threatened. All we really knew of this stranger was his wild claim, and that he'd wolfed down a package of peanut butter crackers.

Then I saw little Alice take Jean Philippe's hand. The new man turned toward Bernadette and put his palms on her shoulder and forehead.

Just like that, her eyes opened.

"Bernadette?" Jean Philippe whispered.

"*Cherie?*" she whispered back.

"You did it," Jean Philippe said to the Lord, his voice reverential. "You brought her back. Thank you, Bondyé! Bernadette! My love!"

I have never witnessed anything like that, Annabelle. One moment she was unconscious, the next she was awake and talking. The others began to stir and take notice. Geri poured Bernadette some water. Nina hugged her tightly. Even rigid old Mrs. Laghari seemed pleased, although she mumbled, "Someone must explain how this happened."

"The Lord did it," Nina said.

The new man smiled. Mrs. Laghari did not.

Eventually, we gave Bernadette and Jean Philippe their privacy and moved to the back of the raft. The stranger followed us. I studied his face. If this was a miracle, he was taking it in stride.

"What did you do to her?" I asked.

"Jean Philippe wished to speak to her again. Now he can."

"But she was nearly dead."

"The distance between death and life is not as great as you imagine."

"Really?" Yannis turned his way. "Then why don't people come back to Earth after they die?"

The stranger smiled. "Why would they want to?"

Yannis made a snorting noise. "Whatever." Then he added: "But Bernadette, you healed her? She's going to be good?"

The man looked off.

"She is not healed. But she is going to be good."

Two

Sea

My watch reads 1:00 a.m. Our fifth night lost. The stars are so thick I can't tell where some start and others end, as if a barrel of glowing salt just exploded in the heavens.

For now, I focus on a single star that sparkles so brilliantly, it's like someone is signaling us. *We see you. Wave. Do something and we'll come get you.* If only. We remain adrift with this magnificent panorama all around us. It has always been a mystery to me, Annabelle, how beauty and anguish can share the same moment.

I wish I were staring at these stars with you, from a beach someplace safely on land. I find myself thinking of the night we met. Remember? The Fourth of July? I was sweeping the floor of a pavilion in the municipal park. You approached in an orange blouse and white pants, your hair tied back in a ponytail, and asked where the fireworks were being launched.

"What fireworks?" I said. And at that instant the first of them boomed in the air (a red-and-white starburst, I remember distinctly), and we both laughed as if you had made them appear just by asking. There were two chairs in the pavilion, and I set them beside one another, and we spent the next hour watching those fireworks like an old couple on their porch. Only when the explosions finished did we say our names.

I remember that hour as if I could walk inside it and touch its edges. The curiosity of attraction, the stolen glances, the voice in my head saying *Who is this woman? What is she like? Why does she trust me this way?* The possibilities of another person! Is there any anticipation on this Earth quite like that one? Is there anything lonelier than being without it?

You were educated and accomplished and tender and beautiful, and I confess, from the moment I saw you, I felt unworthy of your affection. I never finished high school. I had few career options. My clothes were dull and worn out, and my bony frame and straggly hair were hardly attractive. But I instantly loved you, and incredibly, in time, you loved me back. It was the happiest I have ever been and the happiest I imagine I ever will be. Still, I always sensed I would disappoint you in some future way. I lived with that silent fear for four years, Annabelle, right until the day you left me. It's been nearly ten months now, and I know it makes no sense writing. But it nourishes me through these lost nights. You once said, "We all need to hold on to something, Benji." Let me hold on to you, that first hour of you, the two of us staring at a colorful sky. Let me finish my story. Then I will let go of you and this world.

⁓

Four a.m. The others are asleep in contorted positions under the canopy. Some snore with gurgling noises; others, like Lambert, are as loud as a buzz saw. I'm surprised he doesn't wake up the whole boat. Or raft. Geri keeps telling me to call it a raft. Boat. Raft. What difference does it make?

I fight sleep desperately. I am fatigued beyond measure, but when I sleep, I drift into dreams of the *Galaxy* sinking, and I am back in that cold, dark water.

I don't know what happened, Annabelle. I swear I don't. The impact was so sudden, I cannot even tell you the moment I was thrown into the sea. It was raining. I was by myself on the lower deck. My arms rested on the rail. My head was down. I heard a booming noise, and next thing I knew, I was hurtling toward the water.

I remember the splashing impact, the sudden bubbly quiet beneath the surface, the heavy roar when I came back up, everything cold and chaotic as my brain began to process and then scream at me, *What the hell? You're in the* ocean!

The water was rough, and the rain drummed on my head. By the time I got my bearings, the *Galaxy* was a good fifty yards away. I saw dark smoke starting to billow out. I told myself I could still swim back to her, and part of me wanted to, because, even wrecked, she was something solid in the otherwise empty sea. Her decks remained lit, beckoning me. But I knew she was doomed. She began to list, as if lying down for a final sleep.

I tried to see if a lifeboat was being released, or if people were jumping off the sides, but the constant crashing of waves impaired my vision. I tried to swim, but where was I going? I remember things drifting past me, things that had been blown off the *Galaxy* just as I had, a couch, a cardboard box, even a baseball cap. Gasping for breath, I wiped the rain from my eyes and spotted a lime-green suitcase floating just a few feet away.

It was the hard-shell kind that apparently doesn't sink, and I grabbed that suitcase and clung to it. Then I witnessed the *Galaxy*'s final moments. I saw her decks go dark. I saw eerie green bulbs light her frame. I watched her slowly drop, lower and lower, until she sank out of sight and a swooshing wave passed overhead, mopping the surface of her last remains.

I began to weep.

I don't know how long I was in the water that way, crying like a little boy, for myself, for the others who were lost, even for the *Galaxy*, which I felt strangely sorry for. But I tell you again, Annabelle, I had no part in destroying that ship. I know what Dobby wanted, and the things I may have inadvertently helped him plan. But I was thrown into the sea with nothing but the clothes on my back, and I tossed in those frigid waves for who knows how long. Had I not found that suitcase, I would be dead already.

I began to hear voices of other passengers in the water. Some were howls. Others were clear enough to distinguish actual words—*Help me!* or *Please!*—but then, in a rush, the sounds disappeared. The ocean plays tricks with your ears, Annabelle, and its currents are so strong that someone could be a few yards away one moment and gone for good the next.

My legs felt heavy; it was all I could do to keep them moving. I knew if I cramped up, I could not swim, and if I could not swim, I would sink and die. I clung to that suitcase like a frightened child clings to his mother's midsection. I was trembling with cold and my eyes were about to shut for good when I spotted an orange raft, drifting in and out of the waves. Someone on board was waving a flashlight.

I tried to yell "Help!" but I had swallowed so much salt water, it burned my throat to make a sound. I kicked toward the raft, but could not move fast enough while holding the suitcase. I had to let it go. I didn't want to. Strange as it sounds, I felt a certain devotion to it.

But then the flashlight shone again, and this time I heard a voice yell, "Here! Over here!" I released my grip and started swimming, my head above the surface so I could keep sight of the beam. A wall of water rose and crashed. My body twisted wildly and I lost all sense of direction. *No!* I yelled to myself. *Not when I am so close!* I broke the surface just as a new wave hit me again. Once more, I was spun and yanked like a fish on a line. When I resurfaced, I gasped for air, my throat burning. I turned my head left and right—nothing. Then I turned backward.

The raft was right behind me.

I grabbed the safety rope along its side. Whoever had been waving that flashlight was gone. I can only imagine he or she was thrown off by those waves. I tried to look for a body in the water, but another wave began curling into form, so I gripped the rope with both hands, and instantly I was tossed again. I lost all sense of up or down. I squeezed that rope so hard my fingernails broke the flesh of my palms. But when I burst through the surface, I was still holding on.

I pulled myself along the outside of the raft until I found

a handle for boarding. I tried three times to yank myself in. I was so weak, I failed each try. Now another large wave was forming. I didn't think I could hang on through that one. So I screamed into the darkness, a guttural "EYARRRRGGG!" And with every ounce of strength I had left, I heaved myself over the side and fell onto the black rubber floor, panting like a mad dog.

News

ANCHOR: *What you're seeing is the area of the Atlantic Ocean where the luxury yacht the* Galaxy *reportedly went down Friday night, some fifty miles off the coast of Cape Verde. Our correspondent Tyler Brewer filed this report.*

REPORTER: *Miles and miles of vast ocean, as search and rescue teams fly over the Atlantic, hoping for any clues as to what happened on the* Galaxy, *a $200 million yacht owned by billionaire Jason Lambert. The ship sent a distress signal around 11:20 Friday night, reporting some type of event. It is believed to have sunk shortly thereafter.*

ANCHOR: *What about survivors, Tyler?*

REPORTER: *The news is not good. By the time rescue teams reached the area, the* Galaxy *was completely gone. Bad weather and strong currents may have carried debris—and even the bodies of any survivors—miles from the original transmission site.*

ANCHOR: *Have they discovered anything at all?*

REPORTER: *There are parts of the yacht's exterior that rescue teams say they have spotted. We're told the* Galaxy *was constructed of a very lightweight fiberglass that allowed it to* go faster than similar yachts. *Unfortunately, that also made it more susceptible to impact. An investigation is underway.*

ANCHOR: *An investigation into what exactly?*

REPORTER: *Frankly, if there was any foul play involved. There are many things that can happen to a ship at sea. But an event this destructive is quite extraordinary.*

ANCHOR: *Well, for now, our thoughts and prayers go out to the families of those lost—including our own Valerie Cortez and cameraman Hector Johnson, who were reporting from the* Galaxy *when this tragedy took place.*

REPORTER: *Indeed. I'm sure many loved ones still hold out hope that at least some of the passengers survived. But the ocean is cold in these parts. And hopes dim with each passing hour.*

Sea

~~~~~~

Day six. Another strange occurrence to report. This morning, the skies grew thick with clouds and the winds whipped up until they sounded like high-pitched engines. The ocean is deafening in such moments, Annabelle. You must scream to be heard, even a few feet away. The salt water blows across your face and stings your eyes.

Our raft rose and fell, smacking the surface with each drop. It was like riding a bucking horse. We gripped the safety ropes to keep from bouncing out.

At one point, little Alice tumbled loose. Nina dove and grabbed her with both arms as a crash of water soaked us all. She scrambled back with Alice in her grip and started wailing, "Stop! . . . Stop!" I saw Alice reach an arm toward the Lord, who was crouched across the raft, unfazed by any of this.

The man put his hands over his nose and mouth and closed his eyes. Suddenly, the wind stopped. The air went dead. All sounds disappeared. It was like that T. S. Eliot poem, "the still point of the turning world," as if the entire planet held its breath.

"What just happened?" Nevin asked.

We looked around from our various splayed positions on the raft floor, which now seemed to be parked in place. The stranger made brief eye contact, then turned away and gazed over the sea. Little Alice hugged Nina around her neck, and Nina soothed her by whispering, "It's OK . . . we're safe." It was so quiet we could hear her every word.

Moments later, the boat began to gently rock, and the ocean formed small, harmless swells. A light breeze blew, and the normal sea sounds returned. But there was nothing normal about that moment, my love. Nothing normal at all.

⁓

"Are the sharks still following us?" Nina asked as the sun tucked under the horizon.

Yannis peeked over the side. "I don't see them."

We spotted the sharks on our second day in the ocean. Geri says they are drawn to the fish that are attracted to the raft's bottom.

"They were there an hour ago," Nevin said. "I think I saw a fin—"

"I don't understand this!" Mrs. Laghari blurted out. "Where are the *airplanes*? Jason said they would be searching for us. Why have we not seen a single plane?"

A few of us looked down and shook our heads. Mrs. Laghari has been carping on this every day. *Where are the planes?* When we first pulled Lambert into the boat, he insisted his crew would have sent distress signals. Rescue would be imminent. So we waited for the planes. We scoured the skies. Back then, we still felt like Lambert's passengers. That has changed. With each passing sunset, our hope grows depleted, and we no longer feel like passengers of anything. We are souls adrift.

I wonder if this is what dying is like, Annabelle. At first, you are so tightly connected to the world you cannot imagine letting go. In time, you surrender to a drifting phase. What comes next, I cannot say.

Some would say that you meet the Lord.

⌐

Trust me, I have thought about that many times, given the stranger in our lifeboat. I call him a stranger, Annabelle, because if he were truly something divine, he must be as far from me as you can get. We are taught as children that we come from God, that we were created in His image, but the things we do as we grow, the way we behave, what is godlike about that? And the terrible things that befall us? How does a supreme being permit them?

No. The right word is *stranger*, which is what God has been to me. As to who this man truly is, well, the boat remains divided. I asked Jean Philippe about it earlier, when we sat together at the rear of the raft.

"Do you think we're about to die, Jean Philippe?"

"No, Benji. I think the Lord has come to save us."

"But look at him. He's just . . . average."

Jean Philippe smiled. "What did you expect the Lord to look like? Don't we always say, 'If only we could see God, we would know he was real'? What if He has finally given us a chance to see Him? Is it still not enough?"

No, I would say, it is not. I know we had that bizarre moment today. And the small miracle of Bernadette's revival. But as with any miracle left long enough in man's hands, more earthly explanations arise.

"Sheer coincidence," Lambert said this morning when we were discussing it. "She was probably already regaining consciousness."

"Or he roused her awake," Nevin suggested.

The stranger emerged from the canopy, and Mrs. Laghari shot him a look as if she'd figured him out.

"Is that what you did with Bernadette?" she said. "Some sort of trick?"

He cocked his head. "It was not a trick."

"I have my doubts."

"I am quite used to doubt."

"It doesn't bother you?" Nina asked.

"Many who find me begin with hesitation."

"Or they don't find you at all," Yannis said, "and they stick to science."

"Science," the stranger said, looking at the sky. "Yes. With science, you have explained away the sun. You have explained away the stars I put in the firmament. You have explained away all the creatures, large and small, with which I populated the Earth. You have even explained my greatest creation."

"What's that?" I asked.

"You."

He ran his hand along the skin of the raft. "Science has traced your existence back to primitive life-forms, and to primitive forms before those. But it will never be able to answer the final question."

"Which is?"

"Where did it all begin?" He smiled. "That answer can only be found in me."

Lambert stifled a laugh. "OK, OK. If you're so great, get us out of this mess. Make an ocean liner appear. Do something besides talk. How about actually saving us?"

"I have told you all you need for that," the man said.

"Yeah, yeah, we all have to believe in you at the same time," Lambert said. "Don't hold your breath."

The conversation dwindled. The man is an enigma for sure, Annabelle, a source of confusion and sometimes even frustration. But, in the end, he is not the answer. We don't have an answer. When Mrs. Laghari asks "Where are the planes?" I know what many of us are thinking. If planes were coming, they'd have been here already.

⁓

I try to remain positive, my love. I think of you, I think of home, I think of a meal and a pint and a nice, long sleep. Small things. I try to stay active in the boat, moving from side to side, stretching the muscles that I can, but the relentless sun often saps my strength. I never realized how precious shade could be. I am redder than I have ever been, and my skin is covered in small boils. Geri had smartly grabbed a backpack before escaping the *Galaxy*, and it had a tube of aloe in it, but it is not nearly enough for all of us.

We share tiny dabs on our worst spots. Our only escape is to crawl under the canopy. But it is stifling with everyone inside, and you cannot sit up straight. Geri's backpack also held one of those small, handheld fans, and we pass it from one to another, creating a miniature breeze. We shut it off quickly to preserve the batteries.

Fresh water remains our most precious commodity. What we have comes from the "ditch bag" of the raft, which also contained various emergency supplies: a bailer for emptying seawater, fishing line, paddles, a flare gun, things like that.

The drinking water, stored in small cans, is what matters most, and it is nearly gone now. Twice a day, we have been rationing equal amounts into a stainless steel cup. We sip it down, then pass the cup on.

Geri makes sure to fill it up for little Alice. This evening, following the strange wind incident, the child took her portion and crawled along the raft bottom toward the Lord.

"What's that weird kid doing now?" Lambert said.

Alice handed her cup to the stranger, and he swallowed the water in a single gulp. Then he handed it back with a grateful nod. What are we to make of him, Annabelle? Never mind the mysterious things that have happened since his arrival. Would God really drink water before a thirsty child?

Land

LeFleur's heart was pounding. Keeping his back toward Rom, he pulled the plastic bag fully from the pouch. The notebook's front cover was torn in half, and its back cardboard was decayed from salt water that had leaked inside. Was it some kind of log? Or maybe a diary that explained what had happened to the *Galaxy*? Either way, LeFleur thought, he could be holding something of international significance.

And no one knew it existed.

The proper protocol was to replace the bag immediately and call in higher authorities. Pass it up. Step out of the way. LeFleur knew this.

But he also knew the moment he called his bosses, he would be excluded from the process. And something about the raft was gripping him. It was easily the most compel-

ling thing that had ever happened on this job. Montserrat
was nearly crime-free. LeFleur spent many of his days in
stifling boredom, trying not to think of how his life had
come unraveled over the last four years, how his marriage
had changed, how everything had changed.

He blinked hard. Today was Sunday. His boss was off.
No one knew he was out here. He could take a peek inside
this notebook, put it back, and who would know the difference?

LeFleur glanced at Rom, who was facing the other way,
studying the cliffs, then slid the bag into the waistband of
his pants and covered it with his shirt. He rose and walked
down the beach, yelling over his shoulder, "Stay there,
Rom! I'm going to check for any other debris."

Rom nodded.

A few minutes later, LeFleur was alone in a cove. He
kneeled down, putting weight on his knees, and removed
the bag from his waistband. Then he slowly peeled it open,
even as the rational voice inside him said, *You shouldn't be
doing this.*

News

ANCHOR: *Memorial services are being held today for billion-aire investor Jason Lambert, who disappeared along with more than forty others when his luxury yacht, the* Galaxy, *sank in the Atlantic Ocean last month. Our Tyler Brewer has more from the site of today's services.*

REPORTER: *That's right, Jim. The US Coast Guard officially declared the* Galaxy *lost at sea following twenty-six days of exhaustive search and rescue attempts. It is believed that the yacht blew apart after some kind of explosion or impact. The cause remains unknown.*

ANCHOR: *Tyler, the list of those lost is extraordinary, isn't it? A former president, world leaders, captains of industry, popular entertainers.*

REPORTER: *That's correct. Perhaps because of that, there are calls from foreign governments to investigate the cause of this tragedy, to ensure that it was not in some way politically or financially motivated.*

ANCHOR: *But first, I imagine, comes the solemn tradition of funerals, made more painful for the lack of the actual bodies.*

REPORTER: *Yes. Here, at the memorial for Jason Lambert, there will be no casket or gravesite ceremony. He'll be remembered by friends and family, which include three ex-wives and five children. We're told none of them will be speaking, only his longtime business associate Bruce Morris.*

Jason Lambert, of course, was a controversial figure, an extremely wealthy man who seemed to enjoy showing the world his fortune. He grew up in Maryland, the son of a pharmacist, and started his working life as a vacuum salesman. Within three years, he took over the business. He soon leveraged his company to buy others, eventually earned a master's degree in finance, and started his now-famous mutual fund Sextant Capital, which has grown to the third-largest fund in the world. Among other holdings, he owned a movie studio, an airline, a professional baseball team, and an Australian rugby club. Lambert was also an avid golfer.

The Grand Idea was Lambert's final creation. It was hailed by some as visionary, and criticized by others who saw it as a frivolous gathering of the rich and powerful. Of course, no one knew what a dark turn the voyage would take. Jason Lambert, presumed dead at age sixty-four.

ANCHOR: *We should also mention that in addition to the famous names lost at sea, there were workers on that boat, the crew, the service staff, and the like, I imagine?*

REPORTER: *Yes. They should be remembered as well.*

Sea

~~~~~~

Bernadette is gone, Annabelle! She is gone! I must calm down. I must keep my wits. I will write exactly what happened. Someone has to know!

I told you yesterday how the man we call "Lord" merely touched Bernadette's body, and she opened her eyes. We all saw her smiling and whispering to Jean Philippe. He was so happy. He kept saying "This is a miracle! The Lord has made a miracle!" I told you this, no? I'm sorry. I am so rattled, I'm not remembering things clearly.

Last night was an uneasy slumber, the raft rocking on the waves. I was out for maybe four hours. I dreamed of sitting in a barbecue restaurant. The smell was so real, so pungent. But the food never came, no matter how many times I craned my neck to look into the kitchen. Then, suddenly, I heard a customer howl.

I awoke to the sound of Jean Philippe crying.

I rolled over and saw him with his head down, his arms limp by his sides. The "Lord" had a hand on his shoulder. The space between them, where Bernadette had been resting, was empty.

"Jean Philippe," I croaked. "Where is your wife?"

No answer. Nevin was awake, tending his wounded leg. When I caught his gaze, he just shook his head. Mrs. Laghari was awake, too, but she just stared out at the dark ocean.

"Where is Bernadette?" I repeated, rising. "Did something happen? Where did she go?"

"We don't *know*," Nevin finally said.

He pointed at Jean Philippe and the Lord.

"They won't talk."

Three

Land

Leaning against a large rock, LeFleur removed the note-book and examined it closely. Its pages were stuck to-gether, likely from the salt, and he realized this would be a delicate process. But there was writing. In English. He felt his hands shaking. He looked up at the breaking waves and contemplated what to do.

Most of his life, LeFleur had been a rule-follower. He'd done well in school, earned badges in scouts, scored high on his police tests. He'd even thought of leaving Montser-rat for England to train as a constable. He was a good size for law enforcement, tall, broad-shouldered, with a thick mustache that hid his smile and made him appear quite serious.

But then he met Patrice. A New Year's Eve party, four-teen years earlier, part of Montserrat's annual festival that features parades, costumed performers, and a Calypso King competition. They danced. They drank. They danced some more. They kissed at midnight and tumbled passionately into the new year. They saw each other every day for the next few months, and there soon seemed little doubt they would marry.

By summer, they had. They purchased a small house, which they painted yellow, and bought a four-poster bed where they spent a great many hours. LeFleur would smile just watching Patrice walk away from the bed and smile even more watching her walk back. Forget England, he thought. He wasn't going anywhere.

A few years later, he and Patrice had a child, Lilly, and they doted on her as new parents do, taking pictures of every move she made, teaching her nursery songs, carrying her on their shoulders for trips to the market. LeFleur painted their second bedroom a light-pink shade and added dozens of little pink stars on the ceiling. Under those stars, Jarty and Patrice put Lilly to bed every night. He remembered feeling so good during those days, it seemed undeserved, as if someone had accidentally given him a double share of contentment.

Then Lilly died.

She was only four years old. She'd been visiting Patrice's mother, Doris, and that morning they'd gone to the beach. Doris, who suffered from heart issues, had taken a new medication at breakfast, not realizing it would make her drowsy. In a beach chair, under the hot sun, she fell asleep. When she blinked her eyes open, she saw her granddaughter facedown in the surf, motionless.

Lilly was buried a week later. LeFleur and Patrice had been in a fog ever since. They stopped going out. They barely slept. They crawled through their days and fell into their pillows at night. Food lost its taste. Conversation faded. A numbness draped over them, and they would stare for long stretches at nothing in particular, until one would say, "What?" and the other would say, "What?" and the other would say, "I didn't say anything."

Four years passed. In time, to their neighbors and friends, it appeared as if the couple had reached an equilibrium. In truth, they'd become their own private Montserrat, blown apart, existing in ashes. LeFleur shut the door to Lilly's room. He hadn't entered it since. He grew withdrawn, and shook his head whenever Patrice wanted to talk about what happened.

Patrice found solace in her faith. She went to church often. She prayed every day. She spoke of Lilly "being with God" and nodded tearfully when her friends said Lilly was in a better place and never had to worry again.

LeFleur could not accept that. He disavowed God, Jesus, the Holy Spirit, anything he'd been taught as a kid in church. No merciful god would take his child that way.

No Heaven needed his daughter so badly that, at four years old, she had to drown. Faith? What idiocy, he thought. The world to LeFleur became dark and irrational. He drank more. He smoked more. Few things mattered to him. Even the yellow house and the four-poster bed seemed stale. The power of misery is its long shadow. It darkens everything within view.

But this orange raft and its hidden notebook? They were a jolt to that misery. He wasn't sure why. Maybe it was the idea that something—even a few pages of something—had endured a tragedy and crossed an ocean to find him. It had *survived*. And witnessing survival can make us believe in our own.

He carefully separated the front cover from the first page. He saw dense writing. On the inside flap, there was a message scribbled in blue ink.

To whoever finds this—
There is no one left. Forgive me my sins.
I love you, Annabelle DeChapl—

The rest was ripped away.

Sea

~~~~~~

Our eighth day in the raft, Annabelle. Blisters have formed on my lips and shoulders, and my face is itchy with a budding beard. I obsess about food all the time now. It enters my every thought. Already I feel my flesh stretched tighter over my bones. Without food, the body eats its fat, then its muscle. In time, it will come for my brain.

My feet sometimes go numb. I believe this is due to inactivity, and the cramped positions we must sit in to make room for the others. We shift to keep the raft balanced. At times, to stretch our legs, we lay them over one another's, like pick-up sticks. The raft bottom is always wet, which means our bottoms are always wet, which means constant blisters and sores. Geri says we must rise and move around regularly, or risk more sores and hemorrhoids. But we can't all get up at once without tilting the raft, so we take turns; one person walks around on their knees, then someone goes after and someone after that, like exercise breaks in a prison yard. Geri also reminds us to keep speaking, to make conversation, it will help our brains stay sharp. It's difficult. It's so hot much of the day.

Geri was a guest on the *Galaxy*, but in the raft, she is the steadying force. She did some sailing when she was younger and she comes from California, where she spent much time on the ocean. Initially, others looked to Jean Philippe or me for answers, because we worked on the yacht. But Jean Philippe says little now. He is grieving his wife. And I only worked one other boat before the *Galaxy*, as a junior deckhand. I had to learn fire prevention and some basic first aid. But mostly I was cleaning, sanding, waxing. And attending to guests. None of that prepared me for what we are enduring now.

Our last can of water, according to Geri's calculations, will be gone by tomorrow. We are all aware of what that means. No water, no survival. Geri has been working on a small solar still from the ditch bag, a conical plastic thing that is supposed to use condensation to produce fresh water. She set it up so it drags behind the raft on a cord. But so far it has been ineffective. A rip, she says. The truth is, with ten of us, how could it come close to producing enough?

I did just write "ten of us." I realize I have not told you

of Bernadette's fate. Forgive me, Annabelle. I could not bring myself to write it the last two days. The shock took time to absorb.

⁓

It was Mrs. Laghari who finally got an answer from Jean Philippe. He had been silent for hours, softly crying. The Lord, sitting next to him, twirled a raft paddle between his palms.

Finally Mrs. Laghari rose to her knees, still wearing the long pink T-shirt Geri had given her, her salt-and-pepper hair pushed back behind her ears. She is a short woman, but she commands respect. With a determined voice, she said, "Mr. Jean Philippe. I realize you are grieving. But you must tell us what happened to Bernadette. We cannot have secrets. After this man revived her"—she pointed to the Lord—"did he do something else?"

"The Lord did no harm, Mrs. Laghari," Jean Philippe whispered. "Bernadette was dead."

Several of us gasped.

"But she had woken up," Nevin said.

"She seemed fine," I added.

"We thought he healed her," Nina said.

"Wait," Yannis said. "I asked if he healed her, and he said he didn't."

He turned to the Lord. "But you did say she was good."

"She is," the Lord replied.

"She's gone."

"Someplace better."

"You smug bastard," Lambert said. "What did you *do*?"

"Please, stop," Jean Philippe whispered. He put his forehead in his hands. "She was speaking to me. She said it was time to trust God. I said, 'Yes, *cherie*, I will.' Then she smiled, and her eyes closed." His voice quivered. "Didn't she have the most beautiful smile?"

Mrs. Laghari leaned forward. "Did anyone else see this?"

"Alice," Jean Philippe said. "The poor child. I told her Bernadette was sleeping. Just sleeping. Beautiful . . . sleep."

He broke down. Most of us were crying, too, not just for Bernadette but for ourselves. An invisible shield had been shattered. Death had paid its first visit.

"Where's her body?" Lambert said.

I don't know why he asked that. It was obvious.

"The Lord told me her soul was gone," Jean Philippe rasped.

"Wait. He told you to throw her over the side? Your own wife?"

"Stop it, Jason!" Mrs. Laghari barked.

"You dumped her in the ocean?"

"Shut up, Jason!" Yannis snapped.

Lambert sat back, smirking.

"Some God," he cracked.

⁓

This evening, when the sun went down, a group of us were sitting outside the canopy. Nightfall brings fear. It also brings us closest together, as if we are huddled against an invader none of us can see. Tonight, with Bernadette's absence, we seemed particularly vulnerable. A long time passed without a peep from any of us.

Finally, out of the blue, Yannis began to sing.

Hoist up the John B's sails
See how the main sail sets . . .

He stopped and looked around. The rest of us exchanged glances but said nothing. Nina offered a feeble smile. Yannis let it go. His voice is high-pitched and warbly, not something you want to listen to for long anyhow.

But then Nevin shifted to his elbows. He coughed once and said, "If you're gonna sing it, lad, sing it correctly."

He lifted his neck. I could see his protruding Adam's apple. He cleared his throat and sang.

Hoist up the John B's sails
See how the main sail sets . . .

Mrs. Laghari took the next line.

Call for the captain ashore
Let me go home . . .

The rest of us began to mumble along.

Let me go home,
I want to go home,
Well, I feel so broke up, I want to go home

"It's break up," Nevin interrupted. "Not broke up."
"It's broke up," Yannis said.
"Not in the original lyrics."
"How do you feel so 'break up'?" Lambert said.
"Broke!" Mrs. Laghari declared. "Now do it again."
And we did. Three or four times.

Let me go home, let me go home,
I want to go home, yeah, yeah . . .

Even the Lord joined in, although he didn't seem to know the words. Little Alice watched as if she'd never seen such a thing before. Our voices dissipated into the empty ocean night, and at that moment it was possible to believe we were the only people left on Earth.

News

ANCHOR: *As stunned families around the globe hold memorial services for their loved ones, we begin a series of tributes to those who were lost in the sinking of the* Galaxy *yacht last month. Tonight, Tyler Brewer profiles a remarkable woman who rose from abject poverty to one of the most powerful positions in her industry.*

REPORTER: *Thank you, Jim. Latha Laghari was born in the Basanti slums of Calcutta, India. She lived her early years in a cramped shack made of wood and tin. There was no electricity and no running water. She ate once a day.*

When her parents died in a cyclone, Latha was taken in by a relative who sent her to boarding school. She excelled at chemistry and upon graduation was hoping to study medicine, but no scholarships were available to a woman of her background. Instead, she worked for two years at a meatpacking factory to save enough money to travel to Australia, where she found a job in cosmetics production.

Latha's chemistry background and tireless work ethic saw her rise from a product tester to chief development officer at Tovlor, Australia's largest cosmetics company. In 1989, she left to start her own business back in India, which grew into one of the top twenty cosmetics firms in the world, and which now makes the popular Smackers lipstick line.

Interestingly, Latha Laghari wore very little makeup herself. Known as an elegant, no-nonsense businesswoman, she raised two sons with her husband, Dev Bhatt, who made his fortune in the cell phone communications field.

DEV BHATT: *"Latha was the rock of our family. As firm as she could be in business, she was gentle and loving to our children. She always made time for them, and for me. She said our family was the gift she was given for the family she lost as a child."*

REPORTER: *Latha Laghari was seventy-one years old when she was invited onto Jason Lambert's yacht for the star-crossed Grand Idea voyage. She leaves behind a grieving family, a Fortune 500 company, and a Center for Women's Education that she created in Calcutta. In an interview, Laghari once said that, for all the schooling she experienced later in life, her first six years in the Basanti slums taught her the most important life lesson. When asked what that was, she said: "Survive until tomorrow."*

Sea

~~~~~~

Day nine, Annabelle. It is dark, and I am very tired. I tried twice to write you but failed. I am still in shock from earlier today. Death has struck again.

I was resting in the back of the raft when Geri crawled over on her knees. "As long as you have that notebook, Benji," she said, "why don't you make an inventory? We need to keep tight track of our rations."

I nodded OK. Then she turned and asked everyone to bring what we had and lay it out in the middle of the raft. Before long, we were staring at the meager spread of our possessions.

For water, we had only half a can left.

For food, we had three protein bars from the ditch bag, plus items we had pulled from the ocean the night the

Galaxy sank, four bags of cookies, two boxes of corn-flakes, three apples, and the remnants of a box of peanut butter crackers that Geri had thrown into her backpack before jumping ship.

For survival gear, again from the ditch bag, we had two paddles, a flashlight, a throwing line, a knife, a small pump, a bailer, a flare gun, three flares, binoculars, and repair patching kits. Also, one seasickness pill. We'd swallowed the rest in our first two days.

Geri's backpack added a first-aid kit, a small tube of aloe, several T-shirts and shorts, a pair of scissors, sunglasses, her little motorized fan, and a floppy hat.

Finally, there were the random items that we plucked from the waves: a tray, a tennis ball, a seat cushion, a yoga mat, a plastic tub of pens and notebooks—which is how I am able to write you right now—and a car magazine, which, despite having been soaked and dried many times, has been read by nearly everyone in the raft. It reminds us of the world we left behind.

We also had the clothes we were wearing when we escaped the sinking ship: long pants, button-down shirts, Mrs. Laghari's blue gown. Perhaps the material will prove useful.

Nobody spoke much as I recorded the items in my notebook. We knew the food and water would not sustain us much longer. We have made vain attempts at catching fish—from trying to club them to trying to grab them over the raft sides—but without a hook, there is not much chance. I don't know why hooks were not in the ditch bag. Geri says it all depends on who packs it.

Lambert, who was eyeballing the items, suddenly blurted out: "Do you know what my fund did last year?"

Nobody responded. Nobody cared.

"Eight billion," he said anyhow.

"What difference does your money make now?" Nina asked.

"It makes all the difference," Lambert said. "It's my money that will keep people looking for us. And it's my money that will ultimately find whoever destroyed the *Galaxy*. If it takes the rest of my life, I will hunt down the animal who did this to me."

"What are you talking about, Jason?" Mrs. Laghari said. "Nobody knows what happened on the boat."

"*I* know!" Lambert bellowed. "That yacht was top shelf. Every last detail was looked after. There's no way it sinks on its own. Somebody sabotaged it!"

He scratched his head, then looked at his fingers. "Maybe they were trying to kill me," he mumbled. "Well, ha ha, you little pricks. I'm still here."

He looked at me, but I avoided his gaze. I was thinking about Dobby. I was thinking how much we both hated this man.

Lambert turned to the Lord, who was smiling.

"What are you grinning at, Looney Tunes?"

The Lord said nothing.

"For what it's worth, if you really are God, I never called for you. Not once. Not even in the water."

"And yet I still listen," the Lord said.

"Stop talking, Jason!" Nina snapped.

Lambert glared at her. "How did you get on my yacht? What do you do?"

"I style hair for the guests."

"Oh, right," Lambert said. "And you, Jean Philippe, the kitchen, correct?"

Jean Philippe nodded.

"And you, scribble boy. Benji. How come I don't know what I pay you to do?"

I felt his eyes on me. My body roiled inside. I'd worked on the *Galaxy* for five months. He still had no clue who I was. But I knew him.

"Deckhand," I said.

Lambert grunted. "A deckhand, a haircutter, and a cook. Really useful out here."

"Give it a rest, Jason," Geri said. "Benji, you got this written down yet?"

"Almost," I replied.

"I'm just going to say this now," Nina blurted out. "If something bad happens"—she pointed at Lambert—"it's because of him!"

"Yeahhhup. It'll all be my fault," Lambert answered. "Except, hey, look, nothing's happening. Oh, well."

Just then, I noticed the Lord putting his hand over the side of the raft. It dangled in the water. I found that strange.

A moment later, the rubber floor thudded sharply, as if something were trying to punch its way through.

"Sharks!" Geri yelled.

Before we could absorb those words, the floor thudded again. Then, suddenly, the raft shot forward and we all tumbled over. It stopped after a few seconds, spun to the left, then shot forward again.

"They're dragging us!" Geri yelled. "Hold on!"

Everyone grabbed for the safety ropes. The raft surged ahead. Then the front half lifted and I saw the gray-and-white flesh of a massive fish, as if it were trying to tip us over. Geri, Nevin, and Jean Philippe tumbled forward and the goods were scattered, some spilling into the ocean.

"Save the stuff!" Lambert yelled. I grabbed the flare gun and the bailer, and I saw Mrs. Laghari raise up to retrieve the binoculars, which had tangled with her blue gown and fallen into the water. The raft jolted wildly, and she lost her balance and toppled overboard.

"Oh my god!" Nina yelled. "Pull her in!"

I scrambled to the edge but Mrs. Laghari was just beyond my reach, flailing her arms and spitting water. She seemed too shocked to scream.

"Stay still!" Geri yelled. "Let us get you! Don't move!" She grabbed a paddle to pull us closer. Mrs. Laghari kept smacking her arms on the surface.

"Get her NOW, Benji!" Geri screamed. I leaned over with my arms outstretched, but before I could make contact, Mrs. Laghari disappeared in a spray of seawater. It was like she'd been hit by a missile. I fell back in horror. To this moment, I cannot shake that image, Annabelle. She just blew sideways and was gone.

"Where is she?" Nina screamed.

Geri spun left and right. "Oh, no, no, no . . ."

We saw a spread of red blood on the water.

We did not see Mrs. Laghari again.

I dropped onto the raft floor, gasping for air. I couldn't breathe. I couldn't move. I caught a glimpse of the Lord, who held little Alice in his grip. He turned my way as if he were looking right through me.

Four

Land

LeFleur drove with his body slightly twisted. The plastic bag was tucked inside his shirt, and he was doing his best to hide it from Rom. Not that Rom seemed interested. He stared out the rolled-down window, the breeze swirling his wavy hair.

LeFleur had only been able to read the first paragraphs of the notebook. When he tried to turn the page, it tore in his hands. Fearful of doing more damage, he slid the notebook back into the bag. But he had seen enough. The experts were wrong. Passengers *had* survived the sinking of the *Galaxy*. For now, he was the only one who knew.

The raft remained on the beach—it was too large to fit in the police jeep—so LeFleur called two men from the Royal

Defense Force to guard it until the next day, when he could bring a truck. The force was mostly volunteers. He hoped they knew what they were doing.

"We'll stop ahead," LeFleur announced, "grab something to eat, OK?"

"Yes, Inspector," Rom answered.

"You gotta be hungry, right?"

"Yes, Inspector."

"Look, you can stop with the formalities, OK? You're not being investigated here."

That caused Rom to turn.

"Am I not?"

"No. You just found the raft. You didn't do anything to it."

Rom looked away.

"Right?" LeFleur said.

"Yes, Inspector."

What a strange bird, LeFleur thought. The north shore seemed to attract a lot of men like him, thin, raggedy drifters who were never in a hurry. They smoked a lot and rode bicycles or carried guitars. LeFleur often thought of them as lost souls who, for some reason, felt found on Montserrat. Maybe because half the island itself was lost, buried in volcano ash.

They pulled into an open-air restaurant that was part of

a small motel. LeFleur pointed to an outside table and told Rom to take it.

"I'm going to find a bathroom," LeFleur said. "Order whatever you want."

Once inside, he rang the front desk bell. Out from the back came a middle-aged woman with a sweep of black hair across her forehead.

"Can I help you?"

"Listen," LeFleur said, his voice low, "I need a room for an hour or so."

The woman glanced around.

"Just me," LeFleur sighed.

The woman produced a registration form.

"Fill this out," she said flatly.

"I'll pay cash."

She put the form away.

"Also, do you have any paper towels?"

A few minutes later, LeFleur was inside a simple room with a double bed, a desk, a lamp, a floor fan, and some magazines atop a mini fridge. He went into the bathroom, ran water in the tub, then removed the notebook from the plastic bag. He ran the notebook gently through the water, just once, to remove dirt and dissolve the salt that was binding the pages together. Then he laid the notebook on one towel and patted it with another. He slid paper towels in between some pages and pressed down. After a few minutes, he was able to separate the cover and reread the opening sentences:

When we pulled him from the water, he didn't have a scratch on him. That's the first thing I noticed. The rest of us were all gashes and bruises, but he was unmarked.

Who was this stranger, LeFleur wondered? He glanced at his watch and realized how long Rom had been waiting. The last thing he needed was that guy to grow suspicious.

He placed the notebook upright on the desk, then pulled the floor fan over to help dry the pages. He hurried out, locking the door behind him.

At the restaurant, LeFleur saw Rom at a corner table, with a glass of ice water in front of him.

"Did you find what you were looking for, Inspector?"

LeFleur swallowed. "What?"

"The bathroom?"

"Oh, yeah. Found it."

He grabbed the menu. "Let's eat."

Sea

It is dawn, Annabelle. I haven't slept. I've been waiting for enough sunlight to write you again. I remain haunted by the death of Mrs. Laghari, and there is no one here that I can speak to about it. Not the way I can speak to you.

I've been thinking about a memory; it comes to me vividly now. A few days ago, I had dozed off, and when I opened my eyes, I saw Mrs. Laghari combing little Alice's hair with her fingers. She did it gently, unhurried, and Alice seemed to revel in the human contact. The old woman straightened the little girl's bangs. She licked her fingertips and pressed them across Alice's eyebrows. Finally, she tapped the girl's shoulders as if to say "All good," and Alice leaned in and hugged her.

Now Mrs. Laghari is gone. We are nine people left in the

raft. Even as I write the words, I cannot believe it. What's happening to us?

~

I realize I haven't written about how Mrs. Laghari or Alice or any of the others wound up in the raft the night the *Galaxy* went down. The truth is, I don't remember much. I was so exhausted after pulling myself in that I must have blacked out. When I came to, I was on my back, and I felt someone tapping my face. I blinked my eyes to see a short-haired woman staring at me.

"Did you set the sea anchors?" Geri said.

It was surreal, the question, the setting, her face, the faces of people behind her, barely lit by the hazy moonlight. I recognized Jean Philippe and Nina from the staff. The others were so wet and terrified-looking, I couldn't place them. My mouth hung open and I turned my head as if looking at a dream.

"Sea anchors?" Geri repeated.

I shook my head no, and she quickly moved away. I saw her rifling through the ditch bag as the others helped to sit me up. That's when I realized there were eight of us: Yannis, Nevin, Mrs. Laghari, Nina, Geri, Jean Philippe, Bernadette—who was lying under the canopy, her head bandaged—and me.

Geri found the sea anchors, two small yellow fabric

parachutes, and she threw them in the water and tied them through grommets on the raft.

"These will slow us down so they can find us," she said. "But we already drifted a lot."

Nina was crying. "Does anyone know we're out here?"

"The yacht must have sent distress signals. We just have to wait."

"Wait for what?" Mrs. Laghari asked.

"A plane, a helicopter, another boat," Geri said. "We gotta stay alert and use the flares if we see something."

She suggested we get out of any clothes that were holding the cold water, and she gave Mrs. Laghari a large pink T-shirt from the backpack she'd grabbed before abandoning ship. I remember Mrs. Laghari asking Nina to unzip the back of her gown, then requesting we turn away while she struggled to get out of it. Even on a lifeboat, people have their modesty. The explosion had come during a dinner party, and the sight of most of us in dress clothes, now soaked and ripped as we huddled inside a raft, was a grim reminder of how little the natural world cares for our plans.

After that, we were mostly silent, just staring at the heavens, hoping to see an approaching airplane. None of us slept. A few of us prayed. It wasn't until the sky began to lighten that we spotted anyone else. Geri had found a flashlight in the ditch bag, and we took turns waving it like a beacon. Somewhere around five in the morning, we heard a distant yell.

"There," Geri said, pointing, "about twenty degrees to our right."

Up ahead, in the flashlight beam, was a man gripping a chunk of something. As we drew closer, I realized it was actually a piece of the *Galaxy*'s fiberglass hull, and the man clinging to it was the ship's owner, Jason Lambert.

I fell backward, trying to catch my breath. *Not him!* He made a guttural moaning sound as the others struggled to pull his corpulent body into the raft.

"It's Jason!" Mrs. Laghari yelled.

He rolled on his side and vomited.

Geri turned to the horizon, which was coming clear with the daylight. "Everyone look carefully out there! This is our best chance to see if anyone else survived!"

When she said that word, it hit me like a bell chime. *Survived?* We were the *survivors?* No one else? No. I could not accept that. There must be others. In some other raft. In some other part of this angry sea. I thought of Dobby. What had happened to him? Where had he gone? Was he responsible for this disaster?

Geri pulled binoculars from her backpack, and we spread about the raft and passed them around. My turn came. At first glance, through those lenses, every small wave seemed like something alive; you'd swear you saw a dolphin, or a piece of equipment flashing in the chop. Then I saw a spot of something red, and red is not a color you confuse with the ocean.

"I think I see someone!" I yelled.

Geri grabbed the binoculars and confirmed it. She removed a soggy piece of paper from her pocket and ripped off a small corner, then threw it in the water and leaned over to watch it.

"What are you doing?" Mrs. Laghari asked.

"The currents," Geri replied. "See how that paper comes back to the raft? Whatever's out there will come our way if we hold our position."

She had us paddle with our hands against the drift. I watched the red figure draw closer and closer. Finally, Yannis, who now had the binoculars, blurted out, "Oh my god . . . It's a *kid*."

We stopped paddling to look. There, in the coming sunlight, clinging to a deck chair, was a little girl, maybe eight years old. She wore a red dress, and her light brown hair was soaked against her head. Her eyes were open, but her expression was blank, as if she were waiting calmly for something to begin. I imagine she was in shock.

"Hey! Are you all right?" we yelled. "Hey!"

Then *splash!* Geri was in the water. She swam until she

reached the deck chair, then swam back with the girl's arms around her neck.

That's how we discovered Alice.

Who has not said a word since.

⁓

When the sun set and the sky turned an amber shade, Geri rose and made an announcement. "Look, everybody. I know what happened to Mrs. Laghari is awful. But we gotta regroup. We need to focus to survive."

I looked at the Lord. I did not tell anyone about his hand going in the water, or that strange look he gave me. Am I imagining things? Was he in some way responsible for that attack? What kind of God would do that?

Jean Philippe collected what was left of our supplies. We'd lost the binoculars, the sunglasses, and, worst of all, some of the food. The sea anchors are gone. The sharks cut a hole in the lower tubing, so the raft tilts downward and water splashes in repeatedly. One of us must constantly bail it out. Geri is trying to figure how to patch the hole closed, but it may mean going beneath the boat, and nobody wants to do that after what just happened.

"From now on, if those sharks get close, we've got to use these," Geri said, holding up one of the paddles. "You bang them on the snout. Hard."

"Won't that make them mad?" Yannis asked.

"Sharks don't get mad. They only attack when they smell or sense—"

"Stop this! Stop it!" Nina yelled. "We have to say something about Mrs. Laghari! We can't talk about what happens next without saying *goodbye* to her! What's the *matter* with us?"

Everyone went quiet. The truth is, none of us knew Mrs. Laghari well. We don't know anyone well. I was aware from our conversations on the *Galaxy* that she had come from India and had two children and that her work involved cosmetics.

"I liked her," I finally said, for no particular reason. Then the others said they liked her, too. Yannis imitated her accent, and a few of us chuckled. It didn't seem right, laughing, but it felt better than weeping. Maybe laughter after someone dies is the way we tell ourselves that they are still alive in some way. Or that we are.

"Tell us that she's someplace better," Nina pleaded, looking at the stranger.

"She is," he said.

Geri scratched her hair. She glanced at Nevin, whose head was bobbing up and down, like someone fighting sleep.

"Nevin? You want to add anything?"

Nevin blinked hard. "What? . . . Oh . . . yes . . . She was lovely." He sighed and rubbed his wounded thigh. "I'm sorry. I'm afraid I'm not much use."

Nevin's injuries have grown concerning. His ankle is bent at a horrific angle, the result of tripping over a locker on the *Galaxy* deck. The wound on his thigh, which he slashed open on that locker, is bad and not closing. Over the days, it's turned dark red, and we have noticed a foul odor. Geri believes there may be a small piece of metal lodged inside, causing an infection. If so, there is nothing we can do. Not about him. Not about Mrs. Laghari. Not about Bernadette. There is nothing we can do about any of this, I fear, except pray and wait to die.

News

ANCHOR: *Tonight, Tyler Brewer continues his series on the victims lost at sea in the mysterious sinking of the* Galaxy. *In his tenth installment, he profiles a British media executive who changed the face of television.*

REPORTER: *Thank you, Jim. You might not know the name Nevin Campbell if you're American, but in Great Britain there is hardly a popular TV program that doesn't bear his mark. He rose from the ranks of the BBC to start his own streaming service, Meteor, which now has more British subscribers than any other.*

Nevin Campbell took chances in the early days of Meteor, borrowing money to finance expensive productions like The Hill, Cleopatra, *and* Do You Know Sherlock Holmes? *At one point, he had a triple mortgage on his home and rode a bicycle around London because he couldn't afford a car. But the shows he gambled on turned into blockbusters, and Campbell became one of the most successful media figures in Great Britain.*

The Times *of London, just before his untimely death, called Campbell "a kingmaker worthy of Hollywood's biggest moguls. If he blesses your production, you will likely make a fortune. If he chooses you for the cast, you'll become a star."*

Nevin Campbell was born into an accomplished family. His father was the noted literary agent Sir David Campbell, and his mother was a law professor at Cambridge University.

Campbell stood six foot five, and as a student he excelled at the pole vault. He once dreamed of representing England at the Olympic Games, but a fourth-place finish at the trials left him one spot shy. Years later he told CNN, "I vowed to never finish out of the money again."

Nevin Campbell was fifty-six years old when Jason Lambert invited him to attend the Grand Idea voyage. Lambert knew Campbell from a deal they did to get Meteor launched. He was interviewed on the deck of the Galaxy *before the ill-fated journey began.*

NEVIN CAMPBELL: *"I know Jason says we are here to change the world, but I'm afraid that's a bit lofty for me. I'll be happy to listen to the others speak, learn a few things, and perhaps get a tan. My colleagues say I'm too pale from working all the time."*

REPORTER: *Campbell and his wife, Felicity, divorced in 2012. They had three children. At the time of his death, Campbell was engaged to the British actress Noelle Simpson. She posted a message on Instagram thanking the public for their condolences and asking the media to respect her privacy during this difficult time.*

Sea

~~~~~~

We have survived our tenth day at sea, my love. This is due to fate, blind luck, or the Lord in the boat. Honestly, I don't know what to think anymore.

Yesterday was another test. Much of the morning we sat in silence, hearing the waves splash. None of us wanted to speak the obvious.

Finally, Yannis did.

"How are we going to stay alive," he asked, "without water?"

Just the mention of water made me thirsty. I haven't written to you about thirst, Annabelle, because the less I focus on it the better. But it is a powerful need. You never think about it until you can't quench it, and then the thought consumes you. Your lips crave moisture. Your throat feels dry as wood. I try to create saliva on my tongue by fantasizing about beverages, Coca-Cola over ice cubes, or a cold beer filling a tall glass, thoughts so real I can feel the liquid going over my teeth. But that only makes me thirstier. It is a unique suffering to be denied the thing your body most craves. All your concentration funnels down to one thought: How can I get it?

"What about that solar still?" I asked Geri.

"There's a hole in it," she said, shaking her head. "Every time I patch it, it blows again."

Nina turned to the Lord. He was rubbing the dark whiskers on his chin.

"Can't you do something?" Nina pleaded. "I know you want everyone to believe in you first. But don't you see how worried we are?"

He squinted against the sun.

"Worry is something you create."

"Why would we create worry?"

"To fill a void."

"A void of what?"

"Faith."

Nina drew closer to the man. She put out her hands. "I have faith." Jean Philippe scooted over and put his hands on top of hers. "So do I." Little Alice glanced up. Perhaps that made three. I felt a sudden division in the boat, as if we'd been sorted by our beliefs. I suppose, when I think about it, much of the world is separated this way.

"Please help us," Nina whispered. "We're so thirsty."

The man looked only at Alice. Then he closed his eyes and leaned back. It seemed like he was taking a nap. What type of response was that, Annabelle? As I keep saying, he is maddening.

But as he slept, the sky began to change. A ribbon of white clouds grew to large puffs, and those white puffs began to gray and thicken. Soon they blocked the sun.

A few minutes later, raindrops fell. Slowly at first. Then heavier. I saw Lambert tilt his head, his mouth gaping open, swallowing the droplets. Nevin gasped, "Is this real?" Yannis ripped off his shirt and so did Jean Philippe, rubbing the fresh water over their salt-crusted skin. As the shower turned to a downpour, I heard Nina laughing.

"Grab anything that can collect water!" Geri hollered.

I found the notebook tub and dumped the contents under the canopy. Then I raced out to catch the raindrops. Geri was doing the same with the bailer. Jean Philippe held up two empty cans and let the fresh supply splash into it.

"Thank you!" he screamed to the heavens. "Oh, thank you, Bondyé!"

We were so busy rejoicing in the storm, we didn't realize how much water was collecting in the bottom of our raft. I moved my knees and slipped. The plastic box spilled its water everywhere.

"Damn it, Benji!" Yannis yelled. "Get back up! Fill it again!"

Lambert still had his mouth open like a fish, and Nevin, lying on his back, was angling the tray on his lower teeth, funneling rainwater to his lips. I saw Alice smiling; she was soaked from top to bottom.

Then, just as quickly as the storm arrived, it ceased. The clouds parted and the sun returned.

I looked at the plastic box, which was mostly empty thanks to my fall. I turned to the Lord, who was awake now, watching us.

"Keep it going!" I screamed.

"So you believe I created that storm?" he asked.

It caught me off guard. I looked at the empty tub, then said: "If you did, it wasn't enough."

"Wasn't one raindrop enough to prove who I am?"

"Just keep it going!" Yannis yelled. "Give us more water!"

The Lord looked up at the thinning clouds.

"No," he said.

Five

Sea

~~~~~~

Day twelve. The water from the rainstorm will buy us a few more days if we ration correctly. Yannis wanted to gather what was in the raft bottom, but Geri said no, we don't know how much seawater got mixed in. We can't take a chance. Drinking seawater is potentially deadly. It leads to muscle spasms, confusion, and, of all things, dehydration. How strange, Annabelle. So much water everywhere, and all of it undrinkable.

We have also suffered another small casualty. The hand-held fan. It died an hour ago. Geri had been holding it up to little Alice's face when the blades stopped. Most of us were watching, and a few of us groaned. Lambert groaned the loudest.

"You wasted it," he said.

"Shut up, Jason," Yannis said.

Earlier this morning, Geri, Yannis, Nina, Lambert, and I sat outside the canopy while the Lord slept underneath it. We don't stay outside for long, as the sun is brutal. But we wanted to speak where he couldn't hear us.

"Do you think he created that rain?" Yannis whispered.

"Don't be stupid," Lambert said.

"We still don't know how he survived in the ocean," Geri said.

"He got lucky. So what?"

"He gets hungry and thirsty like we do," I said.

"And he sleeps," Yannis added. "Why would God sleep?"

"What about Bernadette?" Nina asked.

"That's hard to explain," Yannis admitted.

"No, it isn't," Lambert said. "What did he actually do?"

"He brought her back to life."

"You don't know that. She could have woken up on her own."

"She did die a day later," Geri said.

"Yeah," Lambert added. "Where's the miracle in that?"

"The rain could be a coincidence," Yannis said.

"Then how come it hadn't rained before?" Nina said.

"But why would God stop it when we needed it most?" I asked.

"Read the Old Testament," Lambert scoffed. "God is

fickle, mean, and vindictive. Another reason I never took to religion."

"You've read the Old Testament?" Geri asked.

"Enough of it," Lambert mumbled.

Jean Philippe crawled out from the canopy, so we stopped talking. He wants to believe what he chooses about his wife's passing. We should respect that.

Meanwhile, I fear Nevin is slipping badly. He is quite pale and his leg wound, despite our best efforts, is only getting worse. An hour ago, when I began writing you, I heard him call my name. His lips were covered with blisters and his voice was feeble and halting.

"Benji . . . ," he croaked, waving two fingers. "Can you . . . come here . . . ?"

I crawled over to his tall, thin body. His injured leg was elevated over the side.

"What is it, Nevin?" I said.

"Benji . . . I have three children . . ."

"That's good."

"I . . . I see you writing in your . . . uh . . . notebook. Might you be able to . . . transcribe a message for them . . . from me, I mean?"

I looked down at my pen and said, "All right."

"The thing is . . . I've not spent . . . the time with them . . . that I should have . . ."

"It's OK, Nevin, you will."

He grunted and forced a small smile. I could tell he didn't believe me.

"My youngest . . . Alexander . . . he's . . . a good boy . . . a bit bashful . . ."

"Yes—"

"Tall, like me . . . married a nice woman, a . . . a history teacher . . . I believe . . ."

He voice grew thinner. He rolled his eyes away from me.

"Keep going, Nevin. What do you want me to write?"

"I missed their wedding," he rasped. "Business meeting . . ."

He looked back at me as if pleading.

"My youngest child . . . I . . . told him . . . it couldn't be helped . . ." His right hand fell limply across his chest. "It could have been helped."

I asked again what he wanted me to write, even though I already knew. He blinked his eyes.

"I'm sorry," he said.

Land

LeFleur entered his house quietly. The sun had already set. He had the notebook tucked into a briefcase.

"Jarty? Where have you been?"

Patrice appeared out of the kitchen. She wore jeans and a lime-green T-shirt that draped loosely on her thin frame. Her feet were bare.

"Sorry."

"You left this morning, you didn't call all day."

"You're right."

"What happened?"

"Nothing. Some junk floated up on the north shore. I had to drive up and check it out."

"You still could have called."

"You're right."

She paused, looking at him. She scratched her elbow. "So? Anything interesting?"

"Not really."

"I have dinner."

"I'm tired."

"I made all this food."

"OK, OK."

An hour later, having finished the meal, LeFleur said he wanted to watch the soccer game. Patrice rolled her eyes. He knew she would. He remembered a time when their communication was kinder, their exchanges tinged with the gentility of love. They had lost that in the wreckage of Lilly's death.

"I'm going upstairs then," Patrice said.

"I won't be long."

"Are you all right, Jarty?"

"I'm fine."

"You're sure?"

"Yeah. If the game's boring, I won't watch the whole thing."

She turned without response and climbed the steps. LeFleur went into the back room, flicked on the television, then carefully removed the notebook from his briefcase. He knew everything he was doing was wrong. Taking this notebook from the raft. Failing to inform the higher authorities. Lying to Patrice. It was as if he had tumbled into a rabbit hole and couldn't stop himself from falling in deeper. Part of him kept pushing to go on, take the next step, learn the secrets of this unexpected entry into his life.

He reread the message on the notebook's inside cover:

To whoever finds this—
There is no one left. Forgive me my sins.
I love you, Annabelle DeChapl—

Who was Annabelle? Did the writer believe this note-book would find its way to her? And how much time did these pages represent? Did someone last days before succumbing to the sea? Or was it longer? Weeks? Months?

Suddenly, the phone rang, and LeFleur jumped like a caught thief.

He checked his watch. Nine-thirty on a Sunday night?

"Hello?" he said tentatively.

"Is this Inspector LeFleur?"

"Who's this?"

"My name is Arthur Kirsh. I'm with the *Miami Herald*, just checking up on something."

LeFleur took a moment to respond.

"What is it?"

"Can you confirm that a life raft from the *Galaxy* yacht

has been found on Montserrat? Did you find such a raft, sir?"

LeFleur swallowed hard. He stared at the notebook in his lap.

He hung up.

Sea

~~~~~~

Nevin is dead.

Yesterday, he turned ghostly pale and slipped in and out of consciousness. He couldn't eat a thing. At times he moaned so loudly, some of us covered our ears.

"Something got in that wound," Geri whispered. "Some metal, or whatever he gashed himself on. The infection can't clear. If sepsis has set in . . ."

"What?" I said, hesitantly.

"He's going to die?" Jean Philippe asked.

Geri looked down. We knew that meant yes.

Little Alice was the first to discover him. Just after sunrise, she tugged at my T-shirt. I thought Nevin was sleeping. But she lifted his hand and it dropped limply. Poor Alice. No child should have to bear witness to what she has seen on this raft. No wonder she doesn't speak.

We had a small ceremony. Nina said a prayer. We sat quietly, trying to collectively cobble together a eulogy. Finally Lambert said, "He was a hell of a programmer."

The Lord rose to his knees. "Surely there is more to say about him than that." He was wearing the white dress shirt Yannis had on when the Galaxy went down. He looked around at all of us.

"Nevin had three kids," I offered. "He wanted to be a good father."

"He had a nice singing voice," Yannis added. "Remember when he sang 'Sloop John B'?"

"Did he love others?" the Lord asked. "Did he tend to the poor? Was he humble in his actions? Did he love me?"

Lambert made a face.

"Show some respect," he said. "The man's dead."

⁓

Last night I had a dream. I was sleeping in the raft when a noise stirred me. I looked up and the horizon was blocked by a giant ocean liner. Its white hull was enormous, dotted with portholes, and its decks were jammed with waving people, like those arriving in New York's harbors at the turn of the century. Only somehow I knew these passengers were from the *Galaxy*. I heard them screaming "Where have you been?" and "We've been looking for you!" In the middle of them all was Dobby, with his long hair and toothy smile. He waved a bottle of champagne, motioning me to come join him.

I awoke with a jolt and squinted into the rising sun. The horizon was empty. No ocean liner. No happy passengers. Just the world's longest straight line, from here to oblivion.

I felt my body physically deflate. At that moment, for some reason, the enormity of death began to hit me. I'm not sure why. I had never focused on dying before, Annabelle. I pushed the idea away. We all know we are going to die, but deep down, we don't believe it. We secretly think there will be a late reprieve, a medical advance, a new drug that staves off our mortality. It's an illusion, of course, something to shield us from our fear of the unknown. But it only works until death presents itself so plainly that you cannot ignore it.

I am at that point, my love. The end is no longer a far-away concept. I imagine all those souls who went down with the *Galaxy*. I picture Bernadette and Mrs. Laghari, now Nevin, all swallowed by the sea. Without rescue, the rest of us will suffer the same fate, we will perish in this raft, or in the water outside it, and one of us will watch the others go first. Man's instinct is to find a way to live, but who wants to be the last to die?

As I was thinking this, I looked up and realized little Alice had crawled over to me. Her eyes were wide and her expression gentle, the way children sometimes look when they first wake up. A minute later, the Lord pulled himself alongside her. He looked at me, too. It made me uncomfortable.

"I don't need company," I said. "I'm just thinking about things."

"Your fate," the Lord said.

"Something like that."

"Perhaps I can help."

I actually laughed. "Why? If I were God, I would have given up on me long ago."

"But you are not," he said, "and I never will."

He crossed his fingers in front of his lips. "Did you know that when I created this world, I made two Heavens?"

"When *you* created this world," I mocked.

"Yes," he continued. "Two Heavens." He pointed. "Above and below. At certain moments, you can see between them."

Little Alice was staring at his face. Why she idolizes him so, I can't say. I don't imagine she understands anything he's talking about.

"Just stop, OK?" I said. "Can't you see we're slowly dying here?"

"People are slowly dying everywhere," he said. "They are also continuously living. Every moment they draw breath, they can find the glory I put here on Earth, if they look for it."

I turned toward the dark-blue ocean.

"To be honest," I said, "this feels more like Hell."

"I assure you it is not."

"I guess you would know, huh?"

"Yes."

I paused.

"*Is* there a Hell?"

"Not the way you imagine it."

"Then what happens to bad people when they die?"

"Why, Benjamin?" he asked, leaning forward. "Is there something you want to tell me?"

I glared at him.

"Get away from me," I said.

Six

Sea

~~~~~~

It is time I wrote about Dobby. You need to know. The world needs to know. I will start by saying I am unaware of what happened to him—though I imagine he is dead along with the others. We did not speak that last night on the *Galaxy*, not after I told him "I won't do it." He was furious. He felt I betrayed him. Inasmuch as he thought I shared his rage, I understand that.

But it was his idea to blow up the *Galaxy*, Annabelle. Not mine. Had he not arrived on my doorstep last summer, shortly after you left me, I would have gone along my way, quietly bearing my resentments.

Dobby was more actuated. As a boy, he argued with our schoolteachers, fought the local bullies, led the rest of us kids down dirt paths on our bicycles, always speeding ahead, taking the turns first. He was a rebel in a boy's medium T-shirt, loud, unruly, his dark hair mussed, his brow often furrowed and his lower lip hanging down, as if constantly being scolded by someone. He and his mother came to Boston two years after we did, after Dobby's father, my uncle, passed away back in Ireland. I was nine. Dobby was eleven. I remember overhearing his mother telling mine, "That one runs with the devil in his shoes."

But Dobby was smart. Incredibly smart. He read all the time, borrowed books from the library and read them as he ate breakfast, lunch, and dinner. He was the reason I took to reading, Annabelle, and writing. I wanted to be more like him. We had little competitions, like who could come up with the most shocking ghost story. He always won. He had a better imagination. He also burned for justice before I knew what the word meant.

I remember once, when he was fourteen, Dobby terrorized these four older kids who were throwing stones at a stray cat. He grabbed some metal trash can lids and hurled them at those kids, all the while screaming "This is how big a stone feels to a cat, assholes!" When they scattered, he gathered that cat into his arms and became a different person, tender and patient. "You're all right now, you're safe," he whispered.

No one in my little world acted like that. How I looked up to him! He was only two years my senior, but at that age, two years defines the leader and the follower. He would greet me with a wink and an exaggerated "What's uppp, Ben-*ji*?" It always brought a smile to my face, a sense that I was connected to someone who would rise above our poor little neighborhood. We were just kids back then. But I idolized him. And those you idolize as a child can hold sway over you years later, even when you should know better.

⁓

"These people are pigs, Benji," Dobby said, when he first read about the *Galaxy* voyage in a newspaper. I was scrambling eggs in the Boston apartment we'd been sharing since he'd showed up broke and drunk and singing "Bella Ciao" in my doorway. I had not seen him in several years. The hair at his temples had turned gray.

"They think they can gather like lords of the planet, decide what's good for the rest of us."

"Yes, well," I said.

"I can't believe you're working this clown show."

"It's Jason Lambert's boat. I work on it. What am I supposed to do?"

"Aren't you disgusted by that guy? He says he wants to change the world. But look at how he treats you."

"Yes, cousin," I sighed.

"Why don't you do something about it?"

I looked up.

"What are you talking about?"

"I have a friend . . ." His voice trailed off. He grabbed the newspaper again, found a paragraph, and read it silently. Then he looked me straight in the eye. His expression was dead calm.

"Benji," he said, "do you trust me?"

"Yes, cousin."

He grinned. "Then *we're* going to change the world."

That's how it began.

Dobby's "friend" was a road manager for rock bands, including Fashion X, which was slated to perform on the *Galaxy* Friday night. Over the years, Dobby had worked as a road crew member with different acts. It was how he earned what little money he had. He was good with musical equipment, and he liked the travel, the action, the fast setups and breakdowns.

I always knew this. What I didn't know was that he was parlaying his roadie connections into a terrible plan that involved me. His idea was to get his friend to employ him for the Fashion X concert, then preload equipment onto the *Galaxy*, including instruments, amplifiers, mixing boards, and one object that looked like it fit in but did not:

A limpet mine.

I did not know what a limpet mine was, Annabelle. I

do now. Dobby told me. It is a naval explosive device that attaches with magnets to the underbellies of boats. Frogmen often affix them to hulls in secret, then blow them up from afar. Limpet mines have been used since World War II. How Dobby got access to one, I will never know.

But apparently he snuck this limpet mine in with the musical equipment. It was Friday afternoon, the last day of the Grand Idea voyage. He asked me to help him carry a drum case along the second deck. When we were alone, Dobby stopped, unlocked the top, and lifted it slightly.

"Look, cousin," he said. Inside I saw a round dark-green device, a foot in diameter and six inches high.

"What is it?" I said.

"Something big enough to take this whole yacht down. And Jason Lambert and his rich friends with it."

I was too stunned to respond. My breathing accelerated. My eyes darted down the corridor. Dobby began whispering about how I could lower him on a rope at night, when the *Galaxy* was anchored, then he'd attach this mine to the hull below the water line, where it could inflict the greatest damage.

I barely heard him. A thrumming sound had started in my head.

"What are you *talking* about?" I finally stammered. "I never—"

"Benji, listen to me. Do you know the effect this will

have? There's a former president on this yacht! There are high-tech billionaires who have been ripping people off for years! There are bankers, hedge-fund guys, and best of all, that pig Lambert. All these so-called Masters of the Universe. We can take them all out. It'll be historic. We are gonna make history, Benji!"

I slammed the top shut. "Dobby," I seethed, "you're talking about *killing* people."

"People who are awful to other people," he said. "Who manipulate them. Exploit them. Like Lambert. You hate him, don't you?"

"We can't play God."

"Why not? God isn't doing anything about it."

When I didn't react, he gripped my forearm. His voice lowered. "Come on, cousin," he said. "This is our moment. For all the crap we put up with as kids. For your mother. For Annabelle."

When he mentioned your name, I swallowed so hard, I thought my tongue went down my throat.

"What happens to us?" I mumbled.

"Well, we're the captains of this idea." He blew out his cheeks. "Captains go down with the ship."

"You mean—"

"I *mean*," he interrupted, squinting at me, "either something's important to you or it isn't. You want to make a statement? Or be a doormat the rest of your life, polishing thrones so rich people can sit on them?"

The thrumming had turned into a pounding in my temples. I felt dizzy.

"Dobby," I whispered. "Do you want to . . . *die*?"

"It's better than living like an ant."

It wasn't until that moment, Anabelle, that I knew he was mad.

"I won't do it," I said, the words barely audible.

His eyes flashed.

"I won't do it," I said, louder.

"Come *onnnn*, cousin."

I shook my head.

I can barely describe the look he gave me then. Sorrow, betrayal, disbelief, like I could not have let him down more if I tried. He held that gaze a long time, his lower lip drooping like it did when he was a boy. Then he closed his mouth and cleared his throat.

"All right," he said. "You are who you are."

He lifted the case, turned his back to me, then walked down the corridor and disappeared through a door. And I did nothing to stop him, my love, nothing at all.

Land

"Jarty?" Patrice yelled down. "Who called?"

LeFleur sighed. He had hoped she was already asleep.

"Nobody," he yelled up.

He heard her footsteps on the stairs. He tucked the notebook in his briefcase and raised the volume on the soccer game.

Patrice appeared in the doorway.

"'Nobody' doesn't call the house on a Sunday night," she said. "Jarty, what's going on?"

He ran a palm across his forehead, squeezing the skin as if trying to lure out an answer.

"OK," he said. "It wasn't just junk that floated up on the north shore. It was a raft."

"What kind of raft?"

"A life raft," he said.

She sat down. "Were there any—"

"No. No bodies. No people." He didn't mention the notebook.

"Do you know what ship it was from?"

"Yeah," he said, exhaling. "The *Galaxy*. The one that went down last year."

"With all those rich people on it?"

He nodded.

"Who just called?"

"A reporter. The *Miami Herald*."

She reached out and touched his arm. "Jarty. Those passengers. The news said they all *died*."

"That's right."

"Then who was in the life raft?"

Sea

~~~~~~

The water today is a thick sapphire shade, and the sky is rippled with cottony clouds. It is two full weeks since the *Galaxy* sank. Our food is gone. So is the fresh water from the storm. Our spirits are hollow and our bodies frail.

I've been thinking about the word *saved*, Annabelle. How this "Lord" refuses to save us. How Mrs. Laghari tried to save the binoculars and fell into the sea. How perhaps I could have saved all those people on the *Galaxy* if I had only stopped Dobby and that limpet mine.

I think back to that final afternoon, after Dobby and I parted company. For hours, my head pounded. My stomach hurt. I was yelled at twice by the crew master for not responding to guests quickly enough. I searched for Dobby every spare moment, looking down the halls, peeking over the rails. I never saw him. It was the final day of the event, and there was so much activity.

Perhaps I was in denial. Perhaps I thought Dobby would never really go through with it. I'd never known him to be a killer. Angry? Yes. Resentful? Yes. He could argue a blue streak about class, wealth, privilege. But a murderer of strangers? Could a person truly change his nature so much? Or is it a case of what you can't imagine, you won't believe?

"Benji?" I heard Jean Philippe say. "Come out of the sun."

He was under the canopy with the others, all except Yannis, who had dragged out to relieve himself over the side. We move so slowly now, like infants crawling.

"Please, my friend," Jean Philippe said. "You are burning." It was midday, the worst time to be exposed. I hadn't realized how long I'd been out there. I slid back toward Jean Philippe until I was just inside the canopy.

Everyone was quiet, their burned and blistered legs extended between one another like logs. Lambert was poking at the car magazine. The Lord caught my gaze and gave me a goofy smile. I turned away and saw, outside, that Yannis was on his knees, staring at the sky.

"Oh my god," he mumbled. "Don't anybody move."

"What?" Nina said.

"A bird."

Our eyes popped open. A bird? Nina rose to peek out, but Geri blocked her with an arm and motioned for her to be silent. We heard a small fluttering sound. Then a shadow appeared on the canopy.

The bird's feet were moving just above us.

"Benji," Yannis whispered, "it's coming toward the edge."

I stared at him and flipped my palms. What did he want me to do?

"When I say so, reach around and grab it."

"*What?*"

"You're the closest. You have to grab it."

"Why?"

"Because it's *food.*"

I began to sweat. I saw the others looking at me. Lambert made an angry face.

"Grab the stinking bird," he said.

"I *can't.*"

"Yes, you can! Grab it!"

"Benji, please," Nina said.

"It's walking to the edge," Yannis said, his voice low and steady. "When I say so . . . reach up and grab its feet."

I was mortified.

"Get ready . . ."

I raised my hands up toward the flap. I tried to imagine

what the bird looked like. I prayed for it to fly away, save itself, save me.

"Here it comes . . . ," Yannis said.

"Easy, Benji," Geri said.

"You can do it," Jean Philippe said.

"I don't want to," I whispered.

"Just *grab it*!" Lambert said.

My hands were trembling.

"Now," Yannis said.

"Wait—"

"Now, Benji!"

"No, no, no," I groaned, even as I shot my hands up and, with one sharp motion, swung them around and slammed them down. I felt the small bumpy talons in my fingers and I squeezed hard. The bird squawked, flapping its wings manically. I spilled out of the canopy, and its feathers whipped my chin as its long white body tried desperately to flee, twisting, yanking, pecking at my fingers. I tightened my grip and squeezed my eyes shut.

"What do I do?" I screamed.

"Kill it!" Lambert yelled.

"I can't! I can't!"

The squawking was horrible. *Have mercy!* it seemed to be screaming. *I am not one of you! Let me go!*

"I'm sorry! I'm sorry!"

"Don't let go!"

"Benji!"

"I'm sorry!"

Then Yannis was on top of me. He snared the bird's head and twisted it fiercely. It died with a snap. Its plumage fell against my chest. Tears were streaming down my cheeks. I looked at the dead creature. I looked at Yannis. I looked at the rest of them, including the man who calls himself the Lord, and all I could blurt out was "Why?"

News

ANCHOR: *Tonight, in his twelfth installment, Tyler Brewer profiles another victim in the sinking of the* Galaxy, *a promising young ambassador cut down in his prime.*

REPORTER: *Yannis Michael Papadapulous was born outside Athens in 1986. His father was the nation's former prime minister, his mother a well-known opera singer. Yannis spent much of his youth traveling, and was sent to the prestigious Choate prep school in Connecticut before enrolling at Princeton and staying in the States to earn an MBA at Harvard.*

He became known for several start-ups in Greece, and launched a vacation rental service that became the most successful booking agency in his country.

Yannis was catapulted to fame when People *magazine, in a special edition dedicated to foreign celebrities, named him Sexiest Greek Man Alive. He was cast in two small films and became a regular presence in international party spots like the Côte d'Azur, Ibiza, and St. Barts.*

His father, Giorgios Papadapulous, insisted Yannis return to Greece when he turned thirty to "get serious with his life."

GIORGIOS PAPADAPULOUS: *"My son was very gifted. Even as a boy, he was able to solve difficult math equations in his head. I imagined if he focused on something like economics, given his natural leadership, he could be a great help to his country."*

REPORTER: *Yannis won his first election to parliament a year later, thanks largely to his celebrity. A few years after that, over objections from other cabinet members, he was named ambassador to the United Nations, the youngest person in Greek history to achieve that status. Critics claimed he was given the job as a political favor to his father. But Yannis became an effective spokesperson, and helped secure international loans to bail Greece out of its serious financial crisis.*

At thirty-four, Yannis Papadapulous was the youngest person invited to join Jason Lambert's Grand Idea voyage. He is presumed dead, his short life and promising career a victim of whatever happened that fateful night at sea.

Sea

~~~~~~

It is nearing midnight on our seventeenth day. I apologize, my angel. I have not been able to write until now. Ever since Yannis snapped that bird's neck, it's like I've been drugged. I don't know why it affected me so. The feathered carcass falling limply against my chest. I can't get that out of my mind. I feel heavy, and can barely pull myself to a sitting position.

Maybe you're wondering what happened next. Nothing. Not for a few minutes anyhow. No one on board seemed to know what to do with that dead bird. We just stared at each other. Finally, Jean Philippe spoke up.

"Miss Geri," he said, quietly, "may I have the knife?"

He then began to skin the creature, plucking off the wings, cutting off the head. Nina cringed and asked if Jean Philippe knew what he was doing. He said yes, he'd had to do this as a boy in Haiti, usually with chickens, but this wasn't much different. He did not seem happy doing it. Perhaps he wasn't happy doing it back then, either.

We shifted away as the blood and guts spilled out. Eventually Jean Philippe cut out the breasts, which were the meatiest part, and sliced them into stringy pieces. He told us each to take one.

"We're supposed to eat it raw?" Lambert said.

"You can let it dry in the sun," Yannis said, taking a piece, "if you want to wait two days."

Yannis began chewing. Nina looked away. Geri took a piece and handed it to little Alice. As has become her pattern, she gave hers to the Lord, so Geri handed her another. Soon all of them were chewing with exaggerated jaw movements. I could not bring myself to do it.

"Please, Benji," Jean Philippe said. "You must eat."

I shook my head.

"Do not feel bad about killing this creature. You did it for all of us."

I looked at him, and my eyes watered. If he only knew the truth. That I did nothing for all of them, not when it mattered.

I glanced at the Lord, who was eating his piece and looking at me the entire time. He swallowed and smiled.

"I am here, Benjamin," he said. "Whenever you wish to talk."

This evening, just after sunset, I noticed Nina and Yannis sitting next to each other. Who you sit next to on this raft means little, given how compact everything is. You are always on top of somebody. It's strange how quickly we've grown accustomed to the cramped space, twisting our backs to allow each other passage, shifting legs so that someone can stretch out. I imagine Lambert, Geri, and Yannis are used to huge rooms in huge houses. How odd this must be for them, no real estate to themselves.

Still, Nina and Yannis were sitting close not for practical purposes but for companionship. Yannis had his arm behind her, resting on the raft's edge. At one point she leaned her head against his shoulder, her long rivulets of hair brushing against his chest. His hand squeezed against her arm, and he kissed her forehead.

I instinctively turned away, out of privacy or envy, I am not sure which. We burn for water, we growl for food. But what we yearn for most is comfort. A soft embrace. Someone to whisper "It's all right. It's all right."

Perhaps Nina and Yannis are finding that in each other. I find it in these scribbled notebook pages, Annabelle, in thoughts descending from my brain to my fingers to the pen to the paper. To you.

I find it in you.

It seems clear now that I will die on these waters. If so, I want the world to know a few paragraphs about me, about my life. I have no reason to expect this notebook will go anywhere that I won't. But when all your big ideas are gone, you cling to the small ones. Perhaps something will happen to bring this story to light.

⁓

Here, then, is my life summation: I am an only child, born in Donegal, Ireland, in the small northern town of Carndonagh, hard by the waters where the Atlantic Ocean and the Sea of the Hebrides converge. My mother, like many Irish kids, used to play golf on a nearby course. She became so good that at age eighteen, for winning a local tournament, she was given a ticket and a bus trip to watch the Open Championship in Scotland. There, I later learned, she met my father, or rather encountered him, because that was also the last she saw of him for years. I was born nine months later. My mother never spoke his name, no matter how often I asked. She also never played golf again. Sometimes, as a child, I heard her arguing late at night with a deep-voiced fellow out in the kitchen, and I thought this might be the man I should call Dad. But he was merely an old flame who might have married my mother had she not gone off that week to Scotland and "ruined yourself." He yelled those words over and over, enough for me, with my head in a pillow, to become permanently ashamed of my existence.

I had an aunt, Emilia, Dobby's mother, and an uncle, Cathal, her husband. One morning, when I was seven years old, they drove my mother and me to the county airport, which had just replaced its grass landing strip with a paved runway. We gave our suitcase to a porter. We flew away.

We arrived in Boston in the middle of a snowstorm. I did not understand the accents and was overwhelmed by the cars and the multitude of billboards that hung everywhere, for Dunkin' Donuts, for McDonald's hamburgers, for various types of beer. We lived in a flat next door to an Italian bakery, and when my mother found a job in a tire plant, I was sent to school. A city school. I did poorly. The teachers were old and distant. They seemed as relieved as I was when the bell rang to end the day.

I never understood why my mother chose that city, or America, until one afternoon when I came home from school and found her standing before a mirror in a tight silver dress that I had never seen before. She had done up her hair and applied her makeup, and it was almost like looking at another woman, that's how startling her sudden beauty was. I asked where she was going, and she just said, "It's time, Benjamin," and I said, "Time for what?" and she said, "Time for me to see your father."

I didn't understand what she meant. America was still

a mysterious country to me, and in my childish imagination, I pictured her going someplace outside the city, high on a hill, where fathers waited in lonely rooms for their long-lost brides to return. She would report to a person at the front desk who would yell out her name to a crowd of anxious men. One of them—handsome, strong, with dark stubble of a beard—would rise and yell "Yes, that's me!" and run to embrace my mother for the answered prayer of her arrival.

It did not go that way.

Whoever the man was, he did not receive my mother well. I was awakened that evening by her smashing things in her room, and I ran in to see her running scissors through the dress she had worn. Her makeup was tearstained, her lipstick smeared, and when she saw me she screamed, "Go away! Go away!" But even then I could tell she was only echoing my father's reaction to her.

She offered few details about him. I learned that he was rich and that he lived in a house in Beacon Hill. My mother tried to insist that he cared about me, but I knew it was a lie. I saw the heartbreak in her eyes as she told it. I understood, at that moment, that she had been planning all my life for that night, to try and make us whole, to try and make us a family, to unruin herself, and that she had been rebuked, an act that, in my mind, cemented my father as forever a bastard, and me, by definition, a bastard as well.

My mother was a contradiction in many ways. Skinny and frail, she had nonetheless uprooted us, by herself, to a strange new country. When her hoped-for rendezvous collapsed, she did what she had to do. She worked tirelessly at that plant, taking overtime, going in on weekends. She had the endurance of five men, I swear. But one day she fell from a scaffold and damaged her spine so badly that she couldn't walk. The plant, trying to avoid a large payment, said in court that she was negligent. My mother had never been negligent in her life.

After that, her spirit waned. She would watch television with the sound off. Sometimes she went days without eating. She never spoke of the plant accident, or what happened with my father, but it was understood that her grand plan for a better life had tried and failed, and that failure hung in the air of the tiny kitchen where we ate our meals, and in our dull-green bathroom, and in the peeling paint and faded carpet of our bedrooms. Sometimes, when we went for walks, with me pushing her in a wheelchair, my mother would cry for no reason; when someone passed with a dog, or when kids were playing baseball. I often felt she stared at things but saw something else. Broken people do that.

My mother's most repeated advice to me was this: "Find one person you can trust in your life." She had been mine for my turbulent childhood, and I tried to be hers in the years she had left. After she died, I felt heavy all the time. My breathing was labored, my posture stooped. I worried that I was ill. I realize now this was merely the weight of love that had nowhere to go.

So I carried that love, searching the world for a place to lay it down, but never found anywhere or anyone until I found you. I have been a poor man in many ways, Annabelle. Perhaps, upon reflection, even an unlucky one. But I was lucky in the most important way. That night after the fireworks, you told me your name and I told you mine. And you looked at me with your eyes wide open and you said, "Benjamin Kierney, would you like to take me out one day?" I was so overwhelmed, I couldn't answer. I think that amused you. You got up, smiling, and said, "Well, maybe one day you will."

The rest of my life seems inconsequential after that— where I worked, what neighborhood I lived in, what I thought about certain things. There was you, Annabelle. Only you. I am near the end of this page and realize I can sum up my life before I reach the bottom.

I am thirty-seven years on this Earth, and I have been a fool for most of them. In the end, I failed you, as I always feared I would.

I am sorry for everything.

Land

LeFleur chugged the remainder of his coffee and killed the engine on his jeep. The morning was cloudless and the forecast was for hot, steamy weather.

As he carried his briefcase to the front door of the station, he was already thinking of what hours he could carve out to continue reading the notebook. He had barely begun when Patrice interrupted him. But he'd read enough to know something strange had happened on that life raft, when they discovered a man floating in the sea:

> *Nina touched his shoulder and said, "Well, thank the Lord we found you."*
> *Which is when the man finally spoke.*
> *"I am the Lord," he whispered.*

LeFleur had been perplexed enough by the mere existence of this notebook—and all the questions it raised about the *Galaxy* sinking—but now he felt compelled to learn the passengers' reaction to this self-proclaimed deity. LeFleur had a long list of issues he would raise with God, should he ever have such an encounter. He doubted God would like them.

He thought about Rom. He'd told him to come by the office around noon. *The guy doesn't even have a cell phone.* As he pushed the station door open, two figures quickly rose to their feet. One was a rather large man in a navy suit and open-collared shirt. The other LeFleur recognized immediately. His boss. Leonard Sprague. The commissioner.

"Jarty, we need to talk," Sprague said.

LeFleur swallowed hard. "My office?" he said. He chided himself for sounding defensive.

Sprague was a puffy older man, bald and bearded. He'd had the job for over a decade. Normally he and LeFleur met at headquarters, every couple of months. This was the first time he had come to LeFleur's place.

"Am I to understand you found a raft from the *Galaxy*?" he began.

LeFleur nodded. "I was just writing up my report—"

"Where?" the other man interrupted.

"Excuse me?"

"Where did you find the raft?"

LeFleur forced a grin. "Sorry, I didn't get your name—"

"Where?" the man snapped.

"Tell him, Jarty."

"North shore," LeFleur said. "Marguerita Bay."

"Is it still there?"

"Yeah. I had the locals—"

But the man popped up and was heading to the door. "Let's go," he barked over his shoulder.

LeFleur turned to Sprague. "What the hell is going on?" he whispered. "Who *is this guy?*"

"He works for Jason Lambert," Sprague said. He rubbed his thumb against his fingers. Money.

Seven

News

ANCHOR: *Tonight, Tyler Brewer completes his tribute series on the victims of the* Galaxy *yacht with a profile of a famous name in swimming who, tragically, was lost to the sea.*

REPORTER: *Thank you, Jim. Geri Reede was most at home in the water. From the age of three, she was swimming at a local pool in Mission Viejo, California. Before she was ten, she was competing in national events. A self-described "pool rat" and the daughter of a swim-instructor mother and an oceanographer father, Geri qualified for the US Olympic team when she was nineteen. She went to the Games in Sydney and won a gold medal in the breaststroke and two silvers in the relay events. She made the team again four years later and captured a silver medal in Athens before retiring from the sport and spending a year as a global ambassador for world hunger.*

At twenty-six, Reede decided to try medical school, but left after two semesters. Describing herself as "restless" without competitive sports, she spent a year crewing with the yacht Athena, *an America's Cup challenger.*

Eventually Reede partnered with a fitness company to create Water Works!, a health-care line for athletes that

blossomed into a hugely successful company. Reede's signa-
ture spiked blond hair and smart if somewhat acerbic style
endeared her to fans, and she became a spokesperson in the
Water Works! ad campaigns.

Although Geri Reede never married or had children, she
often spoke about the importance of early swimming lessons
for kids. "Fear of the water is one of the earliest fears we
have," she once said. "The faster we get over it, the faster we
learn how to overcome others."

Reede was thirty-nine years old when she vanished with
nearly four dozen others aboard the Galaxy.

"Geri was a trailblazer and an inspiration for young
women everywhere," said Yuan Ross, a spokesperson for
USA Swimming. "She was somebody you wanted on your
team, in the pool and in life. Losing her is a tragedy."

Sea

~~~~~~

My dear Annabelle. It's been days since I last wrote you. A weakness has taken hold of my body and my soul. I can barely lift pen to paper. So much has happened, some of which I still cannot accept.

By our nineteenth day, hunger and thirst had completely overtaken us. We'd eaten every part of the bird that was edible. Geri balled up some of the flesh in an attempt at fishing. She fashioned a hook from a small wing bone and dropped the line in the water. As exhausted as we were, we pulled ourselves over to watch.

Then Yannis yelled, "Look!" In the distance, gray clouds were packed together, with a funnel-shaped darkness dropping to the sea.

"Rain," Geri rasped, her voice thin from dehydration. We perked up at the idea of fresh water. But the wind began gusting wildly. The waves increased. We rose and fell and rose and fell, the raft floor slapping with each new bump.

"Grab on to something," Yannis yelled. Geri, the Lord, and I hooked our arms around the safety rope. Lambert ducked under the canopy, as did Nina, Alice, and Jean Philippe. The raft bounced like an amusement park ride. We had not been this tossed since the night the *Galaxy* sank. The skies darkened. We rose sharply. I saw Geri staring over my shoulder. Her eyes widened.

"Hang on, Benji!" she yelled.

I spun in time to see a giant wave opening wide behind us, like the yawning mouth of a water beast. We were sucked up into it and tilted to the edge of flipping. Then an avalanche of white water crashed overhead, and I gripped the rope for dear life. Through the bubbly rush I saw a body shoot out from the canopy and wash over the side.

"Nina!" I heard Yannis yell. A second passed. Two. Three. We flattened out. I heard Nina's voice against the surf, screaming for help. Where was she?

"There!" Geri yelled. "To the left!"

Before I could react, Yannis had hurled himself into the water and was swimming toward her.

"No, Yannis!" I screamed. Another swirl lifted us, and a wall of water slammed down. I wiped my eyes furiously. In the distance I saw Nina's head bobbing up and down. She was a good twenty yards away now. Another wave smashed against the raft. I saw Geri trying to row, and I scrambled toward her, yelling, "Give me the other paddle!" Another crash. Another white shower.

"Where are they?" I screamed, wiping my eyes. "Where did they go?"

"There!" Jean Philippe yelled.

They were off to our right now, but farther away. I saw Yannis finally reach Nina. I saw them grasp each other. Together they went under, then resurfaced. Then another wave hit us. Then another. Then I couldn't see them anymore.

"Geri!" I yelled. "What do we do?"

"Row!" she hollered.

"Where?"

She spun her head. For the first time, she didn't have an answer, because there was no answer. Yannis and Nina were gone from sight. I paddled madly, as did Geri, ripping into the waves that broke on all sides of us. The wind whipped my face so hard that tears streamed down. I could barely see. For all I knew we were spinning the raft around like a record player.

We never found them. After ten minutes, my weak muscles groaned in pain. I dropped back and wailed "NO!" and was soaked by another wave, as if to shut me up. The wind howled. The raft was calf high with seawater. The others held their ropes and stared at the horizon, avoiding looks that said the obvious. Two more taken. Two more gone. I could hear the boast in the ocean's torturous roar. *You will never escape. I will have you all.*

~

No one spoke for hours. The storm passed, the rain never hit us, and the sun returned in the morning like a tireless demon punching in for its daily shift. We stared at our feet. What was there to say? Five dead from this lifeboat, plus dozens lost the night the *Galaxy* went down. The ocean was collecting us.

Lambert mumbled incoherently now and then, something about phone calls and "Security! Call security!" Gibberish. I ignored him. Little Alice was draped over Geri, squeezing her arm. I thought about the morning when Mrs. Laghari straightened Alice's hair, licking her fingers and flattening her eyebrows, the two of them smiling and hugging. It felt like years ago.

And Nina? Poor Nina. From the moment I met her on the *Galaxy*, she looked to believe the best in people, and she went to her death believing the stranger in our boat would save her. He did not. He did nothing. What more proof of his charade do we require? She told me once that she had asked the Lord about prayers. He'd said all prayers were answered, "but sometimes the answer is no."

I suppose it was no for Nina. It infuriates me. When I glare at the man, he returns my look with a placid expression. I can't imagine what he is feeling or thinking, Annabelle. Or if he feels and thinks at all. When we had food, he ate it. When we had water, he drank it. His skin is chafed and blistered like ours. His face is hollow and bonier than when we discovered him. But he utters no complaints. He does not seem to be suffering. Maybe delusion is his best ally. We all search for something to save us. He thinks it is him.

Yesterday morning, I awoke to see Geri fussing with a patching kit.

"What are you doing?" I mumbled.

"I've got to try and patch the bottom, Benji," she said. "We don't have enough people to keep bailing. We'll sink."

I nodded wearily. Ever since the shark attack, which ripped a hole in the lower tube, one of us has been constantly shoveling water out of our tilted raft bottom. It's an endless, tiring task, only tolerable because there were many of us. But Lambert is slow at bailing, and lately he has been out of it. Little Alice tries, but she fatigues quickly. That leaves only me, Geri, Jean Philippe, and the Lord. Even collectively, we don't have the strength anymore.

"The sharks, Miss Geri," Jean Philippe protested. "What if they come back?"

Geri handed him a paddle, then handed one to me.

"Bang 'em hard," she said. When she saw my reaction, she lowered her voice. "Benji, we have no choice."

We waited until the sun was high, when sharks are least likely to be prowling for food. With Jean Philippe and me leaning over the sides, paddles up like two exhausted sentinels, Geri took a breath and dropped into the water.

The next half hour was like sitting in a darkened house, waiting for a killer to reveal himself. Nobody spoke. Our eyes darted across the surface. Geri kept coming up then diving back under then coming up again. She found the hole, which she said was small, but being underwater left the glue and patches useless.

"I'm going to try some sealant and stitch it," she said.

Again, we watched the water intensely. After twenty minutes, Geri said she'd fixed all she could. Then she dove back under one more time.

"What's she doing now?" I asked.

She resurfaced with her hands full of weeds and barnacles. She tossed them into the raft, and we pulled her in.

"There's a whole . . . ecosystem . . . on the bottom of this raft," she gasped. "Barnacles. Sargasso. I saw fish, but they scattered . . . too fast . . . They're living off what's growing on the bottom."

"That's good, right?" I asked. "The fish? Maybe we could catch one?"

"Yeah . . ." She nodded, still panting. "But . . . that's what the sharks are after, too."

⁓

Now, Annabelle, I must share one more thing, and then I will rest. The writing takes a lot out of me. Processing thought. Thinking about anything besides water and food. I helped Geri pump air into the repaired tubing. It took us an hour. Then both of us fell back under the canopy. Even that simple act was draining.

Still. Last night, in a moment of grace, we witnessed something otherworldly. It was after midnight. As I slept, I felt a sensation through my closed lids, as if someone had turned on the lights. I heard a gasp, and I opened my eyes to witness an utterly amazing sight.

The entire sea was aglow.

Patches below the surface were illuminating the water like a million small light bulbs, casting a Disneyland bluish white all the way to the horizon. The ocean was dead calm, as if it had parked itself in place, and the effect was like looking at a massive sheet of glowing glass. It was so beautiful that I wondered if my life had ended and this was what came next.

"What is it?" Jean Philippe whispered.

"Dinoflagellates," Geri said. "They're like plankton. They glow if they're disturbed." She paused. "They're not supposed to be this far out."

"In all my life," Jean Philippe marveled, "I never see anything like this."

I glanced at the Lord. Little Alice was asleep next to him. *Wake up, child*, I wanted to say. *See something astonishing before we die.*

I didn't. In fact, I barely moved. I couldn't. I kept staring at the glowing sea, awestruck. At that moment, I sensed my insignificance more than at any other moment in my life. It takes so much to make you feel big in this world. It only takes an ocean to make you feel tiny.

"Benji," Jean Philippe whispered to me. "Do you think the Lord created this?"

"*Our* Lord?" I whispered, nodding backward.

"Yes."

"No, Jean Philippe. I don't think he created this."

I saw the blue light reflecting in his pupils.

"Something must have."

"Something," I said.

"Something magnificent," he added. He smiled. The raft rocked gently in the water.

The next morning, Jean Philippe was gone.

Land

LeFleur and Commissioner Sprague watched the man in the blue blazer approach the orange raft. LeFleur shifted his shoes in the sand. *There was no way this guy knew about the notebook, right?*

"You think anyone from the *Galaxy* actually made it to that raft?" Sprague asked.

"Who knows?" LeFleur said.

"Crap way to die, I'll tell you that."

"Yeah."

LeFleur's cell phone rang. He glanced at the display.

"My office," he said.

He turned his body and lifted the phone to his ear, keeping an eye on the man by the raft.

"Katrina?" he answered, low-voiced. "I'm busy now . . ."

"There's a man here for you," his assistant said. "He's been waiting awhile."

LeFleur glanced at his watch. *Damn it.* Rom. He had told him to be there by noon. LeFleur watched the blue-blazered man lean into the raft and run his hand across the edges, near the now-empty pouch. Was he stopping? Did he notice something?

"Jarty?" Katrina said.

"Huh?"

"He asked for an envelope. Is that OK?"

"Yeah, yeah, whatever . . . ," LeFleur mumbled.

The man stood up. "We need to transport this thing out of here!" he yelled. "Can you get a truck?"

"Right away," Sprague yelled back. He waved a finger at LeFleur.

"I gotta hang up, Katrina," LeFleur said. "Tell Rom not to go anywhere."

Eight

Sea

~~~~~~

This is what I found in my notebook the morning Jean Philippe disappeared.

Dear Benji—
When you were sleeping, I think a lot. I reach into the water to touch the blue light. Suddenly, I see a big fish. It swims close to the boat. I take the paddle and I wait. It comes back and I hit it hard. I hit it just right. It stop swimming and I grab it.

I feel happy because there is fish to eat. But sad because I kill it. I don't want to be in this world anymore, Benji, taking things. I want the last thing I do to be giving. You and others please, eat the fish. Stay alive. I want to be with my Bernadette. I know she is safe.

I think last night she let me see Heaven. She is saying God waits for me.

I pray you get home. I leave the fish in the bag.

May the Lord protect you, my friend.

I closed the notebook and dropped my head. I cried so hard my chest hurt, but my eyes stayed dry as dust. This is how empty I have become, Annabelle. I have no water left for tears.

~

That was yesterday. When I told Geri, she took the notebook, read the words herself, then handed it back and went straight for the ditch bag.

The fish was large, as Jean Philippe had promised. "A dorado," Geri said. Using her knife, she quickly dissected it into the edible, the useful, and the rest. The five of us ate some right away. (The five of us? Can that really be true?) Then Geri used a piece of line to hang the remaining fleshy pieces. They will dry in the sun and feed us for another day or two.

I was staring at those pieces and grieving for Jean Philippe when the Lord slid over and leaned against the raft edge. His mop of hair was wet and shiny, and his dark beard was now quite thick.

"Did you know about Jean Philippe?" I whispered.

"I know all things."

"How could you let him take his life? Why didn't you talk him out of it?"

He looked me straight in the eyes. "Why didn't you?"

I began shaking with rage. "Me? I couldn't! I didn't know! It was something he decided to do on his own!"

"That's right," the Lord said, softly. "He decided to do it on his own."

I glared at him then, this haughty, deluded stranger who enjoyed acting as if he manipulated the world. At that moment, I felt nothing but contempt.

"If you were really God," I seethed, "you would have stopped him."

He looked to the sea and shook his head.

"God *starts* things," he said. "Man stops them."

Land

LeFleur sped down the island's main road in his jeep. The car with Sprague and the man in the blue blazer followed. Behind them was a truck carrying the raft.

Again, LeFleur's cell rang.

"Yeah, Katrina?" he barked, expecting his office.

"Inspector, this is Arthur Kirsh with the *Miami Herald*. We spoke the other night?"

LeFleur exhaled. He didn't need this now.

"We didn't really speak," LeFleur corrected him. "And I don't want—"

"We have it confirmed that a life raft from the *Galaxy* was found on Montserrat, and that you were involved in its discovery."

"That's not true! I just got a call."

"So it *has* been discovered?"

Damn it, LeFleur thought. Why did these guys always play tricks?

"If you want information, you should speak to the police commissioner."

"Were there any remains? Of any passengers?"

"Like I said, Mr. Kirsh, call the police commissioner."

"You're aware that the Sextant people are sending a team to your island?"

"Who's that?"

"Sextant Capital. Jason Lambert's company. And if I were to arrive there tomorrow, where would I find you?"

"Find the police commissioner," LeFleur snapped. "And don't call me again."

He hung up and checked his watch. Three o'clock. Three hours later than he'd told Rom he'd meet him. It couldn't be helped. LeFleur first had to stop at headquarters and explain to Sprague why he hadn't immediately called him with the news ("It was Sunday, Lenny!") and how he'd discovered the raft in the first place ("A drifter found it in Marguerita Bay.") Sprague wasn't happy. He said reporters would want to talk to that drifter, so LeFleur had better produce him quickly.

"Don't screw this up, Jarty. It could make a big difference to Montserrat."

"What do you mean?"

"Tourism is in the crapper. Who's coming here now

except creepers who want a death tour of the exclusion zone? This is our chance to change that."

"How?"

"By changing the story. Let Montserrat be known for something besides the volcano. This guy was rich, Jarty. All his friends were rich—and famous, too. There'll be a lot of eyes on this."

LeFleur was taken aback. "People died in that raft, Lenny. You don't build tourism off of that."

Sprague tilted his head. "How do you know people died in that raft?"

"I . . . don't," LeFleur stammered. "I assumed—"

"Don't assume, OK? Just bring me the guy who found it."

When LeFleur pulled up to his office, he was thinking about the notebook and the pages he had read. He thought about the stranger on the raft refusing at first to save the others.

I can only do that when everyone here believes I am who I say I am.

LeFleur balked at that part. But then, he'd stopped relying on God right after his daughter died. There was no place in his mind for a benevolent force that wasn't benevolent when it came to a four-year-old. Praying was a waste. Church was a waste. Even worse. It was a weakness. A crutch that let you dump your misfortune on some make-believe scale that would balance when you died and reached a "better" Heaven. What crap. The way LeFleur saw it now, you either ran from a volcano or you stayed and shook a fist at it.

As he entered his office, Katrina was hanging up the phone. She seemed upset.

"There you are. I've been trying to call you!"

"I turned my cell off. A reporter was bugging me."

"The man is gone."

"Rom?"

"He never told me his name. He sat on the porch for two hours. I offered him some ginger beer, and he said OK. But when I brought it out, he was gone."

"Where did he go?"

"I don't know, Jarty. He was barefoot. Where could he go? I tried to call you ten times!"

LeFleur raced out the door. "I'll find him," he hollered over his shoulder. Katrina got worked up easily; he didn't need that now. He hoisted the briefcase into the passenger seat and hopped into the jeep. Rom. He was beginning to wish he'd never met the guy.

Sea

~~~~~~

We saw an airplane today.

Geri was the first to spot it. We are so weak that most of the day we just lie under the canopy, drifting in and out of sleep. Geri had dragged herself to the rear of the raft for another futile check on the solar still. She looked at the sky, guarding her eyes with her hand.

"Plane," she rasped.

"What did you say?" Lambert mumbled.

Geri pointed up.

Lambert rolled over and squinted. When he saw it, he tried to stand, something he hasn't done in days. "Hey! . . . I'm here! I'm here." He tried waving his arms, but they dropped like heavy barbells.

"It's too high," Geri rasped.

"Flare gun!" Lambert croaked.

"Too high," Geri repeated. "Never see us."

Lambert flopped across the raft bottom toward the ditch bag. Geri threw herself in his direction.

"No, Jason!"

"Flare gun!"

"It's a waste!"

I was too exhausted to move. I kept glancing from the two of them to the sky. I could barely make the plane out. It was like a spot shifting through the high clouds.

"They're here for me, damn it!" Lambert yelled. He knocked Geri backward and dumped out the bag.

"No, Jason!" Geri yelled.

But Lambert had the flare gun now. He swung his arm wildly and fired off-balance and the flare shot out sideways across the ocean surface, a hot-pink light that fizzled in the water maybe forty yards away.

"More!" Lambert yelled. "Give me more!"

"Stop it, Jason! Stop it!"

He was on his knees, his fat hands rifling through the items on the floor, knocking them aside in search of another canister. His belly was heaving.

"I'm here, I'm here," he kept babbling. Geri spotted the two remaining flares and dove for them. She pulled them to her chest and scrambled back to the raft edge.

"Give me those!" Lambert bounced on his knees, coming after her. "Give me them now—"

Bam! Out of nowhere, the Lord smashed into him and knocked him backward with the full force of his shoulders. He moved so fast, I never saw him coming.

Lambert groaned in pain. The Lord lifted Geri to her knees, then turned to me calmly and said, "Benjamin. Put the things back in the bag."

I raised my eyes to the skies. The plane was gone.

⁓

I realize I have not written about little Alice. Sometimes silent people go unnoticed, as if their lack of words makes them invisible. But being quiet and being invisible are not the same thing. She is on my mind much of the time. As much as I cannot fathom my own death, it is the potential of hers that haunts me the most.

Back when there were more of us, and we had the energy, we'd discussed where Alice could have come from. Lambert didn't recognize her, but then he didn't know many people on his own yacht, including me. Yannis said that on Friday afternoon, a rock band arrived on helicopters and he remembered seeing children. Maybe she was one of them.

We've asked her many times, "What's your name?" and "What's your mommy's name?" and "Where do you live?" She seems incapable of communicating. Yet she is aware of everything. Her eyes move even faster than ours.

Speaking of her eyes, they are two different colors. One is pale blue and one is brown. I have heard of this condition—Geri knew the name of it, though I've forgotten—but it's the first time I've ever seen it. The effect is that her stare is somewhat eerie.

Mostly that stare is reserved for the Lord. She stays by him, as if she knows he will protect her. I think of the lessons I learned in church, about Jesus and the children and the kingdom of Heaven belonging to them. The priest would often speak that verse, and my mother would rub my shoulders when he said it. I felt, in that moment, sheltered from all evil. There is no faith like the faith of a child. I haven't got the heart to tell Alice it's misplaced.

It is morning now. I'm sorry, Annabelle. I fell asleep with the notebook in my lap. I must be more careful. It could drop in the soggy bottom of the raft and become unreadable. Geri had a plastic bag in her backpack, and I have taken to storing the notebook inside that bag for extra protection. You never know when a wave will soak us. Or when I might not wake up at all.

It's been three days since Jean Philippe left us. We have eaten all the meat from his fish. Geri has brought up more barnacles and weeds from the bottom of the raft, which contain tiny shrimp that we gobble down. They are morsels.

Less than a bite in normal life. But we savor them like a meal, chewing slowly and not swallowing for as long as possible, if only to remind ourselves of what it is like to eat.

Fresh water remains the biggest problem. Geri has tried the solar still a hundred different ways. It will not hold. Without fresh water, we are withering to death. Last night, I opened my eyes to see Lambert's large, meaty back bent over the side of the boat. At first I thought he was vomiting, although none of us have done that in a while. But then I saw his head tilt back and his arm lift up to his mouth. In my sleepy haze, I didn't make much of it. But this morning, I told Geri, and she leaned over to where Lambert was now asleep as if searching for something. Finally, she tapped my arm and pointed. There, partially covered by his left leg, was the bailer.

"He's drinking seawater," Geri whispered.

News

ANCHOR: *There's breaking news tonight in one of the most tragic maritime accidents in recent memory. Tyler Brewer reports:*

REPORTER: *It was nearly a year ago that Jason Lambert's* Galaxy *yacht sank in the North Atlantic Ocean, fifty miles off the coast of Cape Verde. Today, a report from the Caribbean island of Montserrat, some two thousand nautical miles away, claims a life raft from the* Galaxy *washed up on its shores.The raft itself was empty, but marine experts hired by Sextant Capital are examining it for clues as to who might have been in it, and whether it offers any information on what happened to the* Galaxy *that night.*

Forty-four people were believed lost in that tragedy, including world leaders in politics, business, the arts, and technology. Today's discovery has already renewed calls for a search of the waters where the Galaxy *went down. Earlier attempts were blocked by Lambert's firm, Sextant Capital, which called it "a fruitless endeavor that would only lead to more heartache." There were also disputes over who held control of those international waters. It is unclear how today's developments might change that.*

ANCHOR: *Tyler, do we know how the raft was discovered, or by whom?*

REPORTER: *Not at this time. Police will only say it was spotted on the north shore by someone who was on the beach.*

ANCHOR: *And what are the chances that a raft could make it all that way across the ocean?*

REPORTER: *Hard to say. One expert we spoke with said it was extremely unlikely, but that a raft's chances were still much better than those of anyone who'd been inside it.*

Sea

~~~~~~

Death.

Two left now, Annabelle . . .

So much has happened. I wish—

Dear Annabelle . . .

Goodbye, Annabelle . . .

God is small

Land

"What do you want me to do, Lenny? I can't make him appear out of thin air!"

LeFleur banged down the phone. Three days with no sign of Rom. *I should have locked him in a damn motel.* Reporters were clamoring for "the man who found the raft." Short of that, they were swarming LeFleur. A few of them waited at his office every morning.

Sprague had been right about one thing. The interest in this story was crazy. In addition to a former American president and some big tech billionaires who were on the guest list, a rock band, a couple of famous actors, and a TV reporter had also died on the *Galaxy.* They'd all had fans and followers—rabid followers, LeFleur realized, based on the endless phone calls, social media posts, and shouted questions from the press, whose presence on the island increased every day.

LeFleur and his staff had spent many hours combing and recombing the other north-shore beaches for signs of anything else from the *Galaxy*—Sprague's idea, strictly for show. What did they think? Because a raft miraculously made its way across the Atlantic, the rest of the boat would follow?

Of course, one thing had made it to the island that no one knew about. The notebook. LeFleur had hidden it in an old briefcase at home. It was too risky to bring to work. Each night, he would wait until after he and Patrice had finished dinner and got ready for bed. Once she was asleep, he would sneak downstairs and continue the story.

His knotted stomach confirmed that he was breaking the rules—the strict ones of police protocol, and the unwritten ones of a trusting marriage. But the notebook had narcotized him. He fell into a spell when he read it, and he needed to know how it ended. The pages were delicate, and deciphering the handwriting was tedious. Doing it after midnight made it that much more fatiguing. He had started taking notes, keeping charts for the actions of each of the eleven people on that raft. He searched old news articles about the *Galaxy*'s passengers, trying to match the names to the account and ensure that this wasn't some crackpot fantasy that a delirious passenger had made up.

He justified that as the reason to keep it secret. The whole thing could be a hoax, and, if so, what would revealing it accomplish? Only confusion and heartache. This was the story he told himself, and the stories we tell ourselves long enough become our truths.

⁓

That night, LeFleur asked Katrina if she could drive him home. He wanted to get a drink, and the police jeep drew too much attention.

"OK," she said, rising. "You coming?"

"Drive your car around back."

As he waited for her to pull around, he glanced at the photo on his desk: Patrice and Jarty swinging Lilly above a beach towel. Each parent held a hand as Lilly lifted her feet in the air, her face pure joy. Patrice loved that picture. LeFleur had, too. But every time he looked at it now, he felt further away from his daughter, as if a rope had been cut and she was drifting off in space. Four years? She'd been gone from this world as long as she'd been in it.

Katrina dropped him at a rum shop not far from his house. This way he could walk home. He took a chair and ordered a beer and glanced around at the locals, some of whom were playing dominoes. He recognized a few, and nodded their way. It was a relief to be away from the foreign media people. LeFleur's mind drifted to the notebook story and the man writing it. Benji. Benjamin. A deckhand. Not one of the famous passengers. None of the reporters was asking about him.

Suddenly, the door swung open and a man walked in. LeFleur knew immediately he wasn't local. The way he dressed, black jeans and boots. The way he looked around. They made brief eye contact. The man sat by the window. LeFleur hoped he wasn't another journalist trying to blend in with the locals so he could wander over and ask "innocent" questions.

LeFleur sipped his beer. Twice he caught the man looking at him. That was enough. He laid a few bills on the table and walked out, catching a good look at the stranger as he did. Fair complexion. Long stringy hair, slightly gray. A lined face that suggested years of hard living.

LeFleur's house was six blocks away. He knew Patrice would be waiting. He walked slowly, breathing in the warm night air. His phone sounded, a text message. He pulled it from his pocket to read:

Any luck finding that guy? —Len

LeFleur exhaled deeply. As he walked, he thought he heard a second set of footsteps. He stopped. He turned.

The street was empty. He continued walking. There it was again. He spun around. Nobody.

He was two blocks from home now, so he quickened his pace. Again, he heard the footsteps, but resisted looking. Let whoever it was get closer first, so he could identify them. As he came around the corner, his yellow house was just ahead. LeFleur felt his muscles tighten. He was bracing for a confrontation when he heard a man's voice say, "Excuse me?"

He turned. It was the guy from the rum shop.

"Excuse me? . . . Inspector, right?"

He had a slight accent that LeFleur couldn't place.

"Listen," LeFleur said, "I told the other reporters everything I know. If you want more information—"

"I'm not a reporter."

LeFleur looked the man up and down. He was panting, as if the six-block walk had tired him out.

"I knew someone. On the *Galaxy*. He was my cousin."

The man exhaled deeply.

"My name is Dobby."

Nine

Sea

~~~~~~

My dear Annabelle. I am so sorry. Have I frightened you?

I see my last page. It was mostly scribble. I don't even remember when I wrote those words. Weeks ago, perhaps. The mornings and nights roll drearily into one another now. Given all that has happened, this is the first time I've felt the clearness of mind to write you.

I have been surviving on barnacles and small shrimp that cling to the raft bottom. A fish actually flopped into the boat one morning; that was food for three days. A recent rain shower allowed two cans to be filled with precious drinking water, which I am rationing, but it's enough to rejuvenate my cells, my organs, my mind. The body is an amazing machine, my love. With just the smallest nutrition, it can clank back to life. Not full life. Not the life I once knew. Not even the life I had grown to know with the others in this lifeboat.

But I am here. I am alive.

Such a powerful sentence. *I am alive.* Like the trapped miner still breathing in the hole, or the man staggering out of a house fire. *I am alive.*

Forgive me. My thoughts go to strange corners. Things are different now, Annabelle. We are still adrift in the vast Atlantic Ocean. There is still nothing but deep water for miles. The Lord still sits a few feet away, trying to comfort me.

But I survive on such meager intake because there is no one to share it with anymore.

I am alive.

The others are gone.

How do I explain? Where do I begin?

Perhaps with Lambert. Yes. I'll start with him, because everything starts with him, and all the things that start with him seem to turn bad in the end.

When I last shared news with you, I wrote that he had been drinking seawater. Geri warned us against this, many times, but I suppose at some point Lambert could not help himself. He was parched and all around him was water and more water, and he is used to taking what he wants. He waited until dark, found the bailer, and apparently gorged himself on the ocean as he had gorged himself on so many things in life.

The effect, after several nights, was noticeable. Lambert changed. He grew incoherent. As Geri explained it to me, seawater is four times as salty as regular water, and since our bodies are constructed to balance things, we try to pee the extra salt away. Except we can't. So the more seawater you drink, the more water you actually expel, while retaining the salt in your body, which means you dehydrate even faster than lying thirsty under the sun. With dehydration comes a system meltdown. Your muscles weaken. So do your organs. Your heart speeds up. Your brain gets less blood, which can make you crazy.

And I suppose, looking back, Lambert did go crazy. He mumbled to himself. He became lethargic and semiconscious. Then, one hot morning, we woke to the sound of his voice screaming, "Get off my boat!"

He was standing over the Lord with a knife to his head.

～

"Get off my boat!" He yelled this repeatedly. The sun was not fully up, and the sky was fuzzy streaks of deep blue and orange. The waves were choppy, the raft unsteady. Drowsy and weak, I blinked several times before I realized what was happening. I saw Geri rise to her elbows and cry out, "Jason! What are you doing?"

Half of the canopy lay sliced on the raft floor. For some reason, Lambert had cut it into pieces.

"Get off . . . my BOAT!" he screeched again. His voice was as dry as the rest of him. He swung the knife back and forth in the Lord's face. "You are . . . useless! Useless!"

The Lord did not seem frightened. He raised his palms in front of him, as if urging calm.

"Everyone here is useless!" Lambert railed. "None of you got me home!"

"Jason, please," Geri said, getting to her knees, "you don't need a knife. Come on." I saw her eyeing little Alice protectively, moving to a space between Lambert and the girl. "We're all worn out. But we're gonna be OK."

"Be OK, be OK," Lambert mocked, singsongy. He spun to the Lord. "Do something, you IDIOT! Call for HELP!"

The Lord, too, glanced over at Alice to make sure she was safe, then looked back at Lambert.

"I am your help, Jason Lambert," he said softly. "Come to me."

"Come to you? Why? To do . . . *nothing*? Anyone can do nothing! Look! We ALL can do nothing! . . . You don't exist! You are useless! You do nothing!"

His voice dropped to a whisper. "I don't believe in you."

"But I believe in you," the Lord said.

Lambert's eyes fluttered closed. He turned away, as if bored with the conversation. For a moment I thought he might topple over and pass out. Then, so fast I can barely remember it happening, he whipped himself backward, his arm outstretched, and slashed the knife across the Lord's neck.

The Lord reached for his throat. His mouth opened. His eyes widened. As if in slow motion, he fell backward over the raft edge and dropped into the ocean.

"No!" Geri screamed. I literally stopped breathing. I couldn't even blink. I stared like a mesmerized animal as Lambert yelled "Done!" and dropped the knife. Geri dove for it and pulled it underneath her, but as she did, Lambert thumped across the raft, grabbed little Alice, and heaved her over the side.

"Out we go!" he bellowed. "Out we go!"

I heard Alice splash into the sea, and my heart pounded so loudly it filled my eardrums. In an instant Geri jumped overboard to go after her, leaving Lambert alone with me. He rose to his unsteady feet and began lumbering my way.

"Bye-bye, Benji!" he screamed. I could not move. It was as if I were watching myself from behind. He rumbled toward me, his bloodshot eyes and beard-covered lips and yellowed teeth and purplish tongue—all of it so near I felt he was going to swallow me whole. He lunged for my head, and at the last instant, out of cowardice more than courage, I dropped as if the air had gushed out of me, and he stumbled over my body and belly-flopped into the sea.

My chest heaved. My head pounded. Suddenly I was alone in the raft. I spun left and right. I spotted Geri catching up with little Alice, who was flailing in the waves, the currents having carried her maybe ten yards away. I heard Lambert slapping the water on the other side, groaning incoherently. I could not see the Lord anywhere.

"Benji!" Lambert spit out. "Benji, *help* . . ."

It was the first time I'd ever heard him use that word. I saw his thick frame fighting the demon below the surface, the one pulling at his heels and cooing, *The end has come, don't fight it.* I could have left him to that demon. Perhaps I should have, given how aloof he'd always been to my very existence. I saw him go under, then resurface. A few more seconds, and he would be gone for good. No more of his selfish anger. No more ridicule. And yet . . .

"Benji," he moaned.

I jumped over the side.

⁓

I had not been in the water since the night the *Galaxy* sank, and it was jolting. My legs had grown so weak from lack of use that just churning them took extraordinary effort. This was probably why Lambert, withered by his dehydration, couldn't navigate even the short distance back to the raft. I splashed my arms toward him. He saw me but did not reciprocate. His eyes were glazed and his lips were open, and I saw him gulp a mouthful of seawater and barely have the strength to spit it out. I grabbed his right arm and threw it around my neck. He was so heavy, I didn't know if I could get us back to the raft. It was like towing a refrigerator through the chop.

"Come on," I urged. "Kick . . . It's right there."

He mumbled something, his left arm flapping weakly on the surface, like a dying fin.

"Benji," he moaned.

"I'm here," I rasped.

"Was it . . . you?"

I stared at his face, just inches from mine. His eyes were pleading. My legs were giving out. I couldn't hold him any longer. Suddenly, without explanation, he slipped his arm from mine and pushed me back.

"Hey, no!" I spat out as he drifted away. I splashed toward him. He went under. I inhaled a breath and submerged to try and lift him; he was even deader weight now. I finally raised him above the surface, but his eyes were closed and his head rolled back. He wasn't breathing.

"No!" I yelled. I tried pulling him by the shirt, grabbing for his shoulder, for his neck, but he kept slipping from my fingers. Then I heard Geri scream.

"Benji! Where are you?"

Geri. Little Alice. Who would help them back in? With no passengers to weigh it down, the raft was drifting away. I looked over my shoulder, but there was no sign of Lambert now, and no sign of the Lord. The orange raft was the only thing breaking up an endless panorama of water and sky.

So I swam, with my lungs bursting, until I reached its edge. I tried to pull myself in, remembering how hard this had been the night the *Galaxy* sank. It was even harder now. I had used my depleted strength going after Lambert. Every muscle from my toes to my jawbone felt unresponsive.

Pull, I told myself. I tried. I slipped off. *Pull! Inside is life. Outside is death. Pull!* With a final yank I lifted myself to neck level, then flopped onto my shoulder, the weight of my body depressing the raft enough for me to fall forward, until the heft of my torso slid me down. I had to lift my legs in with my hands, that's how exhausted they were. But I hit the raft bottom and was never happier to feel any surface beneath me.

I heard Geri weakly calling my name, and I scraped across the floor to the side where she and Alice were bobbing in the water.

"Take her, take her," Geri panted. Little Alice's expression seemed a reflection of my own, mouth agape, eyes wide and horrified. Geri pushed her up, and my trembling hands pulled her in. She fell onto her back.

"Are you OK, Alice?" I shouted. "Alice? Are you OK?"

She just stared at me. I turned back to Geri, whose arms were resting on the ocean surface, her head down like a marathoner who had just finished the race and was considering the enormity of the distance run. I was flushed with admiration for this woman. At every turn she had shown such strength, such courage, the kind of courage I only wished I could possess. For a moment, even amid the horror, I felt a wave of hope, as if, with her help, we might somehow survive this.

"Come on, Geri," I said. "Get back in."

"Yeah," she panted, raising her arms. "Gimme a hand."

I steadied myself against the side, pulling the safety rope around my waist. I reached out to her.

Suddenly her expression changed. She convulsed, her head jerking forward.

"What?" I said.

She looked down, then looked up at me, as if confused. Her head tilted and her arms flopped weakly into the water, as if she'd been unplugged. Her body fell sideways. Her eyes rolled back.

"Geri? . . . ," I yelled. "*Geri?*"

A blossoming pool of red began darkening the sea

around her. Her torso rose briefly to the surface, but not her legs.

"GERI!"

That's when I saw two blurry gray shapes circling for the rest of her. My body shivered in recognition, as all of Geri's warnings came rushing back. *Don't splash. Don't draw attention. Don't stay in the water for any duration.* The sharks had never left. They'd just been circling, as if waiting for us to make a mistake.

I turned away in shock. I heard a thrash in the water, and covered little Alice so she wouldn't see it, or hear it, or remember it. I prayed that the beasts would be satisfied with just one of us. It's horrible to say, but at the moment, that was how I felt.

As I held little Alice, I began to weep with the realization of all that had happened in a few terrible minutes. Everyone was dead. Everyone was dead but the child and me.

"I'm sorry!" I sobbed. "I couldn't save them!"

She studied my tears with a sadness that cut right through me.

"They're all gone, Alice! Even the Lord."

Which is when the little girl finally spoke.

"*I* am the Lord," she said. "And I will never leave you."

Ten

Land

"My name is Dobby."

LeFleur's heart took off like a jackrabbit. Dobby, the guy from the notebook? Dobby, the guy with the limpet mine? Dobby, whom the author had called "mad" and "a killer"? Sentences jumped to LeFleur's mind. *I can see why Dobby wanted him dead . . . It was his idea to blow up the* Galaxy.

"What do you want?" LeFleur asked, his throat suddenly dry. They were squared off on the pavement, maybe thirty yards from LeFleur's yellow house. When Dobby didn't answer, LeFleur added, "I live on this street. All the neighbors know me. They're probably watching through their windows right now."

Dobby glanced at the homes, as if confused, then turned his focus back on the inspector. "My cousin," he said. "His name was Benjamin Kierney. He was on the *Galaxy*. A deckhand. I was hoping maybe you knew what happened to him. Something more than what they told us, anyhow."

"Who's they?"

"The people from Sextant. The ones who owned the boat."

"What did they tell you?"

"Nothing helpful. 'All were lost. We're so sorry.' The standard crap."

LeFleur hesitated. What kind of game was this guy playing? He knew what happened. He was the one who did it. Was he feeling out LeFleur to see if *he* knew? Should he arrest this man right now? On what charge? And with what? He had no gun, no cuffs. He didn't know how dangerous the guy was. *Stall. Find out more.*

"It was just a raft," LeFleur said.

"Were there signs of life?" Dobby asked.

"What do you mean?"

"Any clue that someone had been in it?"

LeFleur collected his breath.

"Look, Mr.—"

"Dobby."

"Dobby. That raft had to travel two thousand miles to get here. That's two thousand miles worth of waves, storms, wind, sea life. What chance would anyone have against all that? For a year?"

Dobby nodded, as if hearing something he'd already told himself.

"It's just that . . ."

LeFleur waited.

"My cousin. He found a way to get through things. He had a tough life. Really poor. He could've given up many times. But he didn't. When I read about the raft, I thought maybe, crazy as it sounds, he found a way to survive that, too."

"You flew all the way down here to find that out?"

"Well . . . yeah. We were really close."

A car turned down the street, its headlights sweeping across them. LeFleur scrambled to the left, Dobby to the right. Now they were on opposite sides of the pavement. LeFleur racked his brain for more details from the notebook. He needed to get back to it, to learn everything about what part this Dobby had really played.

An idea formed in his mind. Risky. But what choice did he have?

"Where are you staying, Mr. Dobby?"

"In town. A guesthouse."

LeFleur glanced at his porch, and the lantern that illuminated it.

"Would you like some supper?" he asked.

An hour later LeFleur was sipping Patrice's goat water soup and forcing a smile as Dobby talked. Patrice had taken it in stride. Her husband had come home with a foreign traveler. Could they add a chair at the table? It wasn't something that happened often, but privately, she welcomed it. The isolation they'd endured since Lilly's death had settled like a shadow inside their house. Any new visitor was a light.

"What part of Ireland are you from, Dobby?" Patrice asked.

"A town called Carndonagh. It's way up north."

"Did you know they call Montserrat 'the Emerald Isle of the Caribbean'?"

"Is that so?"

"Because it's shaped like Ireland. And a lot of people who came here years ago were Irish."

"Well, I left Ireland when I was a kid," Dobby said. "I grew up in Boston."

"When did you leave Boston?" LeFleur asked.

"When I was nineteen."

"College?"

"Nah. I wasn't much for school. Neither was Benji."

LeFleur felt as if a character from a book had come to life. He knew things about this man that the man himself had not yet revealed. He had to be patient, draw him out.

"What did you do after that?"

"Jarty," Patrice said, tapping his hand. "Maybe let the man eat?"

"Sorry."

"Nah, it's all right," Dobby said, chewing on a roll. "I did a lot of things. Odd jobs. Traveled around. Wound up in the concert business."

"You're a musician?" Patrice said.

"I wish." Dobby smiled. "I carry the equipment. Set it up. Break it down. A roadie, for want of a better word."

"How fun," Patrice said. "You must meet a lot of famous people."

"Sometimes, yeah. Famous people don't do much for me."

"What about the army?" LeFleur said. "You ever serve?"

Dobby's eyes narrowed. "Now why would you ask me that?"

"Yes, Jarty," Patrice added. "Why would you?"

LeFleur felt a flush. "Dunno," he mumbled. "Just curious."

Dobby leaned back and ran a hand through his long, stringy hair. Then Patrice said, "Is there a Mrs. Dobby somewhere?" and the conversation shifted. LeFleur silently cursed himself. He'd have to be more careful. If Dobby suspected that LeFleur knew what he'd done, he could disappear from the island before LeFleur could make a case. On the other hand, he couldn't just arrest the man without evidence. Evidence meant the notebook. The notebook meant explaining why he'd taken it. His

thoughts marched around this triangle so intensely he lost
the flow of the conversation, until he heard his wife say,
". . . our daughter, Lilly."

LeFleur blinked hard.

"She was four," Patrice said. She placed her hand on her
husband's.

"Yeah," he mumbled.

"I'm truly sorry for you both," Dobby said. "There's no
words for that."

He shook his head as if lamenting a common enemy.

"The damn sea," he said.

⁓

That night, after dropping Dobby at the guesthouse,
LeFleur parked across the street and killed his engine. Part
of him did not want to take his eyes off of this man.

His phone buzzed. A text. Patrice.

We need coffee. Pick some up.

LeFleur bit his lip. He texted her back.

Having a drink with Dobby. Home in a bit.

He pressed send and sighed. He hated lying to Patrice.
He hated the chasm that was now between them. The latest

chasm. Deep down, he'd also resented that his wife had seemingly made peace with Lilly's death while he was still at war with it. She believed it was God's will. *Part of his plan.* She kept a Bible in the kitchen and read from it often. When she did, LeFleur felt as if a door had been locked that he couldn't get past. He had been a believer earlier in his life, and the day Lilly was born, he did feel blessed by something larger than all of them.

But after her death, he viewed things differently. God? Why turn to God now? Where was God when his mother-in-law fell asleep in her beach chair? Where was God when his daughter got swept into the sea? Why didn't God just make her little feet run the other way, back to safety, back to the house, back to her mother and her father? What kind of God lets a child die that way?

There was no comfort in invisible forces, not for LeFleur. There was only what got put in front of you and how you dealt with it. Which is why this notebook had so engrossed him—and at times frustrated him. A group of shipwrecked people think they have God in the boat? Why not pin Him down? Hold Him accountable for all the horrors He allowed in this world? LeFleur would have.

He clicked open the glove compartment and took a long swig from the whisky flask. Then he reached over the seat for his briefcase, found the notebook, flipped on the courtesy lights, and returned to the story. He didn't notice, in the guesthouse's second-story window, the small round lenses of the binoculars that Dobby watched him through.

⁓

It was after midnight when LeFleur finished the final page.

I am the Lord. And I will never leave you.

He dropped the notebook in his lap. *The little girl was the Lord?* He searched for more pages that weren't there. *The little girl was the Lord.* Storywise, it explained certain things. Why she was always giving her rations to the stranger. Why she didn't speak. She was watching them the whole time. She was watching over Benji. But who was the man who claimed to be God? And why was he allowed to die? Why didn't the little girl save him—or the rest of them?

He glanced at his watch. After midnight. The date on his display had just changed. April 10.

He froze.

Lilly's birthday.

She would have been eight years old today.

He pressed his fingers to his forehead and covered his eyes with his palms. His mind flooded with memories of his daughter. Putting her to bed. Making her breakfast. Holding her hand as they crossed a street in town. For some reason, he found himself thinking about the last scene in Benji's story, the little girl in his arms, and what that little girl might have looked like. He pictured her as Lilly.

He got out of his car, walked to the back, and popped open the trunk. He pulled aside a pale-blue blanket that covered the spare tire. There, wedged inside the rim, was something he had hidden three years ago. A small stuffed animal: Lilly's brown-and-white kangaroo. He'd put it there the night Patrice was gathering Lilly's things in boxes. He hid it because he didn't want every piece of his child to be packed away. He chose that toy because he'd given it to Lilly for her fourth birthday. Her final birthday.

"Daddy," Lilly had said that day, pointing to a slit in the kangaroo's belly, "baby kangaroos go in here."

"That's right," LeFleur said. "It's called a pouch."

"Is the baby safe in the pouch?" Lilly asked.

"The baby is always safe with its mommy."

"And its daddy," she added, smiling.

Remembering that moment, LeFleur broke down. He sobbed so hard, his legs buckled. He squeezed the kangaroo close to his sternum. They hadn't kept her safe. It was all their fault. He thought about the words of the little girl in the notebook: *I will never leave you.*

But Lilly had.

News

ANCHOR: *Another new development in last year's tragic sinking of the* Galaxy *yacht. Tyler Brewer has the details.*

REPORTER: *Following the news that a raft from the* Galaxy *has been discovered on the Caribbean island of Montserrat, the families of the victims have renewed their call to search the ocean for any remains. Today, Sextant Capital, Jason Lambert's former company, announced that a salvage effort will begin immediately. Bruce Morris is Lambert's former business partner, who has since taken over the firm.*

BRUCE MORRIS: *"We believe the recent news warrants a fuller exploration of the fate of the* Galaxy. *We have partnered with Nesser Ocean Explorations, the world's top deep-ocean exploration company, to search the area where we last heard from the* Galaxy, *and to send down probes to the seabed. If there's anything to be found, we will find it."*

REPORTER: *Morris has cautioned that these efforts are often unsuccessful. And even if something were discovered, it's unlikely that it would answer all the questions. But pressure*

from various governments and influential families has ratch-
eted up since that life raft appeared on Montserrat.

ANCHOR: *Speaking of that, Tyler, has the man who discovered the raft been found?*

REPORTER: *Not as of yet. The media here ask about him
every day. But so far, no response. It's a rather small island.
So it seems unlikely someone could go unseen for very long.*

Land

"Good morning!" LeFleur said cheerily when the guest-house door swung open. "Wanna go for a ride?"

"What time is it?" Dobby grumbled, rubbing his face.

"Around eight. I'm heading to the beach where we discovered the raft. I thought you might want to see it."

Dobby sniffed deeply. He wore a black Rolling Stones T-shirt and orange running shorts.

"Yeah," he grunted. "Actually, I would. Can you give me a few minutes to get cleaned up?"

"Sure. I'll be in the jeep."

LeFleur had arrived with a plan. It began with getting Dobby alone, then confronting him with what he knew. He didn't want to run into any reporters. And there was one place where he knew that wouldn't happen.

An hour later LeFleur was steering his jeep through the darkened landscape of the exclusion zone as Dobby gazed out the window. Gone was the lush green vegetation and sherbet-colored houses of the northern side of the island, replaced by a moonlike terrain of mud and gray dunes. Occasionally the top of a streetlight or the upper half of a house could be seen poking up from the ash.

The exclusion zone was the dead half of Montserrat, a dull, empty panorama suggesting the end of one world and the beginning of another. Twenty-four years after the Soufrière Hills eruption, the area remained off-limits.

"Why are there no other cars on this road?" Dobby said.

"Only authorized vehicles."

"The beach is beyond this?"

"Yeah," LeFleur lied.

Dobby looked out the window. "How long ago did that volcano explode?"

"Nineteen ninety-seven."

"I bet you never forget that year."

"No," LeFleur said. "We never do."

Eventually, the jeep reached Plymouth, once the largest town on the island. Four thousand people had lived here. Shops and restaurants had thrived. Now, like Pompeii, Plymouth was defined by its ashen ruins. Oddly enough, it remained the island's official seat of government, but its population was zero, making it the world's only ghost-town capital.

"This is bloody awful," Dobby mumbled.

LeFleur nodded, but kept his eyes straight ahead. Bloody awful, it was. But worse than the calculated murder of a yacht full of innocent people? He didn't get this Dobby, the way he reacted to things. If the notebook was accurate, then Benji's "cousin" was incredibly good at hiding his crimes—and his guilt. But the biggest question still remained: How did Dobby get off the *Galaxy*? How did he escape when everyone else was lost?

"Is that a church?" Dobby asked, pointing.

LeFleur slowed the jeep and saw the remains of a cathedral. "It was," he said. He thought for a moment. "Do you want to take a look?"

Dobby seemed surprised. "All right. If you've got time."

Moments later they were entering the ruined structure, which had been burned inside and out from the volcanic eruption. Light spilled through the exposed beams that once held up a roof. Some pews still lined up parallel to each other, but others were destroyed, their loose boards and rails scattered where they came apart. The floor was covered in ash. Prayer books lay open and abandoned. Here and there some green growth was spreading, the Earth reclaiming the space.

The remains of a lectern, with four steps leading up to it,

stood in the center, before a large archway that was burned black.

"Go stand in that," LeFleur suggested, "and I'll take a picture."

Dobby shrugged. "Nah, that's OK."

"Go on. When else will you be here?"

Dobby hesitated, then shuffled his boots along the ashen ground to the steps. LeFleur waited. Beads of sweat formed on his hairline. The lectern itself was inside a round enclosure, waist high, with a railing all around. One way in, one way out.

When Dobby reached the top, he rested his arms on the dirty edges. Had he been a priest, he'd have been ready for a sermon.

"Lemme grab my camera," LeFleur said. He reached slowly around his side, took a breath, then pulled his gun from its holster. With both hands holding it steady, he aimed the barrel straight at Dobby, whose eyes widened in shock.

"Now," LeFleur said. "What did you do to the *Galaxy*?"

Eleven

Land

"What are you talking about?" Dobby yelled. "Why are you doing this?"

LeFleur's arms were shaking. He kept the gun aimed straight ahead.

"You're responsible for all of them," he said.

"All of who?"

"The people on the *Galaxy*. You killed them all. You brought a mine onto the boat, and somehow you detonated it. Now you're going to tell me how you did it, and how you escaped."

Dobby's face contorted so severely that LeFleur was sure it was an act.

"I don't understand you, man!" Dobby said. "Come on. *Please*. Put the gun down! Where are you getting this from?"

"Are you denying it?"

"Denying what?"

"Are you *denying it*?"

"Yes. Yes! I'm denying it! Jesus, come on. I don't know what you're talking about. Tell me!"

LeFleur blew out a mouthful of air. He freed one hand from the gun and reached for the briefcase he'd carried into the church. He produced the tattered notebook and held it out as Dobby stared.

"I found it in the raft," LeFleur said. "It's all there."

⌒

For the next three hours, as Dobby crouched inside the lectern, LeFleur sat on a pew and read the pages of that notebook out loud, holding the gun in his lap. Periodically, he checked Dobby's face for a response. At the start, he seemed incredulous, but as LeFleur continued, Dobby's shoulders slumped and his head dropped lower.

LeFleur read to him about the sinking of the *Galaxy*. He read about the death of Bernadette, and Nevin, and the cruel fate of Mrs. Laghari. He emphasized the parts about Lambert, his haughtiness, his gluttony, his ego. He went slow and deliberate about the limpet mine in the drum case. Twice he read the part where Benji said, "We can't play God," and Dobby replied, "Why not? God isn't doing anything about it." When he read Dobby's quote about dying in an explosion being "better than living like an ant," he paused like a lawyer letting a damning point sink in.

Throughout the reading, Dobby sighed; at times he chuckled, and more than once he teared up. Now and then he would bury his head in his hands and sigh, "Oh, Benji." Some of his reactions seemed odd to LeFleur, but then the whole scene was odd, reading the notebook of a dead cousin in a destroyed church, talking about God appearing in a lifeboat.

It was midafternoon when LeFleur finished. He had been so engrossed in reading the pages, he'd barely noticed the time. When he read the final line, where the little girl named Alice said "I am the Lord. And I will never leave you," LeFleur closed the notebook and used his sleeve to wipe ashy sweat from his forehead. He stood up, the gun still pointed at Dobby.

To his surprise, Dobby immediately made eye contact. He did not seem rattled, or caught. Rather he seemed subdued with sadness, as if he'd just walked out of a funeral service.

"That's a cry for help, man," he said quietly.

"What are you talking about?"

"He's delirious. He made it all up. Come on. Do you honestly believe he was in a boat with God? You're a cop."

"That's right, I am," LeFleur said, shaking the notebook. "And this has you loading a bomb onto the *Galaxy*, giving a reason, and going off to murder all those innocent people."

"Yeah," Dobby said, almost smiling. "That's the most unbelievable part of all."

"Oh, really?" LeFleur paused. "Why is that?"

"Because," Dobby said, exhaling, "I've never set foot on that boat."

News

ANCHOR: *Tonight, an update on the search for the* Galaxy, *the luxury yacht that sank more than a year ago in the North Atlantic Ocean. Tyler Brewer reports.*

REPORTER: *Thank you, Jim. I'm with Ali Nesser, the owner of Nesser Ocean Explorations in Naples, Florida. In a few days his search vessel, the* Iliad, *will be scanning the Atlantic Ocean where the* Galaxy *is believed to have sunk. Mr. Nesser, can you explain how this process works?*

ALI NESSER: *Certainly. First we map out what's called a "search box"—an area maybe five miles by five miles—based on last known signals and sea currents. In that search box, we'll tow a side-scan sonar and a magnetometer, which measures any change in the magnetic field and sends back images in real time. Basically, we'll keep scouring the area, hoping to pick up a signal of something sizable, like a sunken yacht. If we don't get a signal, we'll widen the box. If we do get a signal, we'll send a probe down for a better look.*

REPORTER: *Is there any chance you could raise the ship?*

ALI NESSER: *That's something you'd have to ask the folks who are paying for the search.*

REPORTER: *But is it possible?*

ALI NESSER: *Anything is possible. I'm not sure why you'd want to.*

REPORTER: *Well, as you know, many well-known people died in that disaster.*

ALI NESSER: *Yes, and that ship is their grave. Do you really want to disturb it?*

REPORTER: *I suppose that's for someone else to decide.*

ALI NESSER: *I suppose so.*

REPORTER: *Reporting live, I'm Tyler Brewer. Jim?*

Land

Dobby put his hands above his head and slowly rose from the lectern.

"I gotta stand up, please," he pleaded. "My back is killing me."

LeFleur kept the gun pointed, but he, too, was getting tired. The reading of the notebook had been draining. He realized this wasn't the most well-thought-out plan, coming to the exclusion zone to pry out a confession. He had no backup. If something went wrong, he was a long way from help.

"I'm still waiting for an answer," LeFleur said. "How did you do it? *Why* did you do it?"

Dobby lowered his hands to the filthy podium. He pushed some ash away with his fingers. "Look," he said.

"I don't really want to tell you all this. But I can see it's the only way you're going to believe me."

"You're gonna say you were never on that yacht?"

"I never was. I *saw* it. I'd gone with Benji to Cape Verde, and I drove him to the docks the morning they loaded up. I was worried about him. He'd been through a lot, and he was acting strange. Agitated. I didn't want him to be alone."

"Why go to the docks?" LeFleur asked.

"This manager of Fashion X was supposed to be there. I wanted to say hello. To be honest, I was hoping he'd hire me for their next tour. That's all. I swear."

"So you saw the *Galaxy*?"

"I saw it. It was a beast, just like he wrote. A monument to greed and excess."

"Now you sound like the man in the notebook."

"I'm just telling the truth. The upper deck was like an outdoor theater, a stage, dozens of chairs, a massive sound system. And every guest on that yacht had a staff member assigned to take care of them. Whatever they wanted, the staff person had to provide. Drinks. Towels. An iPad in the middle of the night. That's how that whole trip worked. At least that's what Benji told me. He had four people to look after from start to finish. I was standing next to him when they signed in."

"You remember who they were?"

Dobby scratched his chin and looked down. "Yeah," he said. "Now I do."

"Who?"

He sighed. "One was Geri, the swimmer. One was the Greek guy, Yannis. One was the Indian woman, Mrs. Laghari—I remember her, because she looked at my clothes like they were offensive, and she asked Benji to hold a pair of earrings for her—and the last was the tall British guy, I forget his name."

"Nevin Campbell?" LeFleur said.

"Yeah. Those were Benji's people. He was assigned to those four."

LeFleur shook his head. "Come on. You just named four people who *happened* to wind up in the lifeboat?"

"I know," Dobby replied. "And I might as well tell you the rest. I met Jean Philippe and Bernadette, too. Benji introduced me. They were nice. Funny."

"What about Nina, the Ethiopian woman?"

"We never met. But I saw her."

"How did you know it was Nina?"

"Trust me, you don't forget a woman like that. She looked like Iman, that model? She waved at Benji, and I said, 'Who's *that*?' He said, 'Nina. She gave me this haircut.'"

LeFleur exhaled. This was crazy. Dobby had just rattled off nearly all the passengers in the story. It was too simple. He could easily be reciting their names, making up his own tale as he went along.

"The little girl?" LeFleur asked. "Alice?"

"Never saw her."

"What about Jason Lambert?"

Dobby bit his lip and looked away.

"What?" LeFleur said.

"Put down the gun, Inspector. And I'll tell you a story."

LeFleur held steady.

"Come on," Dobby said. "You know, in your heart, you don't believe that notebook. Put down the gun, and I'll explain everything."

LeFleur rubbed his eyes with his left hand. "Why do I need a whole story? What's the big deal about Jason Lambert?"

Dobby lifted his gaze.

"Benji thought Lambert was his father."

⁓

As the sun split its rays through the church's broken ceiling, Dobby told LeFleur the story of Benji's childhood.

"Benji's mother's name was Claire. My mother was Emilia. They were sisters. Very close sisters. When my father died, we came to America, just like Benji wrote. But he didn't explain *why* we came.

"Benji's father was supposedly an American, that's true. And his mother did meet him in Scotland, the week of that golf tournament. And like a lot of women in our poor little town, she found herself pregnant too young. She never breathed a word to anyone except my mom. But once she started showing, Claire's parents were ashamed. It was one thing in our community when people knew who the father was. They had someone to blame. But keeping the father secret made it harder for Claire. People acted like it was her fault. It was terrible, the way they treated her. She was smart. A good athlete. But once she gave birth, she was on her own. And Carndonagh was not an easy place to be on your own.

"She raised Benji by herself, working in a butcher shop during the day, living in a flat above it at night. They barely had a penny. The town looked at them as potlickers. Claire wouldn't take any help from her folks. She was proud, even a bit headstrong, to be honest.

"One night, according to my ma, Claire came by, all worked up. She said she'd read a story in a magazine about Benji's birth father. He was hugely successful now and lived in Boston. Claire said she was going to find him, tell him about their son. She believed he would take responsibility. Of course my ma told her, 'Don't be daft. He'll cast you off like a beggar.' But Claire was convinced. She and Benji moved in with us for almost a year, so she could save what she earned and use it for plane tickets. That's when Benji and I got really close. We shared the same bed, ate our breakfasts together. We thought of each other as brothers, because we didn't have brothers of our own.

"Anyhow. You read what happened. They went all the way to the States, and my mother was right. The guy rejected her. Claire was broken. My mother sensed it from her letters and phone calls. That's why we moved to Boston, to be near her. They had a strong sister thing, those two, stronger than work, stronger than country. Funny, 'cause Benji and I kind of developed the same bond.

"Anyhow, by the time we got there, Benji was a changed kid. He knew he'd been rejected. He saw what it did to his mother. He started to hate anyone with money, or anyone who acted superior to him. I guess he associated them with the father he wasn't good enough for. But that father was always in his head. As teenagers, we used to sneak into the bleachers at Fenway Park, the baseball stadium, and he'd look down at the people in the expensive seats and say, 'Any one of those guys might be my deadbeat dad.' Or we'd take the T line after school and ride out to Beacon Hill, the fancy neighborhood, and we'd smoke cigarettes and watch men coming home from work in their nice suits, and he'd say the same thing. 'Might be that guy, Dobby. Or maybe that guy . . .'

"I told him to stop wasting his time. It wasn't worth it. Don't get me wrong. I had plenty of issues with the rich. But not like Benji.

"Then his mom got injured at the factory, and he quit school to take care of her. That was a raw deal. She did nothing wrong. A scaffold she was on collapsed, but that factory built a case against her so they wouldn't have to pay lifetime health coverage. Imagine getting too injured to walk, and then being blamed for it. No wonder Benji was angry.

"I came back to visit them once. I was in the navy at that point, and Aunt Claire was in her wheelchair—it was the last time I saw her alive. Benji was still going on about why she was even working in that factory, and where was the father who should have been responsible for them? He said he'd go after the bastard himself if he ever knew who he was. But Claire took that secret to her grave."

He paused. "Or so I thought."

LeFleur looked up. "What?"

"My ma had moved back to Ireland. A few years later, she got cancer. I was with her one night, near the end, when she told me something she'd sworn to never tell anyone. She said that Benji's father wasn't only rich, but he'd become a pretty famous businessman. And that poor Claire had to read about him in the American newspapers."

He hesitated. "And that his name was Jason."

LeFleur blinked hard, his thoughts racing.

"Lambert?" he said.

"I have no idea. Whatever his last name was, my mother couldn't remember it. She died a month later."

"So how did Benji—"

"I told him! Ahhh!" Dobby howled and rolled his eyes toward the roof. "Stupid! Stupid! He was going on about things. Why he was so poor. Why he never got a break. He was in bad shape, and I felt sorry for him. But when he started in on his deadbeat dad again, I told him to stop, he was never going to find the guy, and even if he did, nothing would happen. That's when I shared what my mother had said. I blurted it out. He just stared at me, dumbstruck."

"When was that?" LeFleur asked.

"A month before he started working on the *Galaxy*. He must have sought Jason Lambert out. Rich guy? From Boston? Right name? Honestly, I never even *thought* about a possible connection—until you read me those pages. But I see it now. Because Benji was so distraught."

He dropped his head into his hands. "Jesus. It all makes sense."

"Wait. You're saying he was so mad at his father—"

"I never said Lambert was his father—"

"He was so mad at a guy named Jason that he decided to blow up a yacht? To get revenge? Come on."

"You don't understand. He was desperate over—"

"What about the mine? Are you saying you never told him how a limpet mine worked?"

Dobby sighed. "Years ago. I was telling him a navy story. I can't believe he remembered that."

LeFleur adjusted his grip on the gun and wiped sweat from his forehead with the back of his hand.

"This is all too convenient," he said.

Dobby thought for a moment. "Maybe not. Did you ever hear of something called confabulation?"

"No."

"I knew a musician who went through it, years ago. It's when someone confuses something they imagined for a real memory."

"That sounds like lying to me."

"But it's not lying. The person honestly believes what they're saying. It can happen when someone has a really bad trauma."

"A trauma."

"Yeah. Like losing a loved one. Or getting blown off a ship and trying to survive in the ocean. The experience makes you believe things you know aren't true.

"All that time Benji wrote that he was talking to me, he must have been talking to himself, doubting himself, torturing himself—"

"Stop!" LeFleur interrupted. "So Benji didn't have a father. Lots of kids don't. They don't sink a yacht to make up for it."

Dobby locked his hands behind his neck and stared into the sunbeams.

"You're missing the point, Inspector."

"What point?"

"Who was he writing to? Who's that whole story directed to? What's the name on the front of that notebook?"

Dobby looked straight at the inspector. "Don't you see? This isn't about Jason Lambert. It's about Annabelle."

LeFleur squeezed his eyes shut. His shoulders slumped.

"Annabelle," he mumbled. "Right. So where do I find *her*?"

"You don't," Dobby said. "She's dead."

Twelve

Land

The ride back was mostly silent. As the sun fell, the exclusion zone took on an eerie grayness. LeFleur never liked being here late. It was ghostly enough during daylight hours.

"You understand I'll have to hold you in custody," he said. "Until I can check your alibi."

Dobby looked out the window. "Yeah. I get it."

"I'll have to charge you with something."

"Whatever."

"What should I charge you with?"

Dobby turned. "You serious?"

LeFleur shrugged.

"How about drunk and disorderly?" Dobby said, looking away. "I can do that if you're buying."

"Fine."

LeFleur was so tired, he had to blink his eyes open as they drove. The adrenaline rush of the afternoon had evaporated, and his body felt like it had been hollowed out. His hands shook on the wheel.

At this point, he didn't know what to believe. Dobby had an answer for everything, but he'd heard the whole notebook before having to explain himself. Was he that clever? That quick with a lie? Or was it Benji, the author, who was delusional? And perhaps responsible for the *Galaxy*'s destruction?

Dobby had mentioned Annabelle, but after saying that she'd died from a rare blood disease and that Benji had struggled to find money for her treatment, he offered no more details. His patience for gunpoint had expired. "I'm not saying any more until you swear I'm not a suspect. I can prove I wasn't on that yacht. Just get me back and let me make some calls."

LeFleur reluctantly agreed. What choice did he have? Deep down, he hoped Dobby *was* telling the truth. He didn't care to be this close to a man who could lie that well.

"You never told me how you found that raft," Dobby said.

"I didn't find it."

"Who did?"

"A guy. A drifter."

"Where is he?"

"That's what everyone wants to know."

"Did he have a name?"

"Rom Rosh."

Dobby turned. "Rom Rosh?"

"What?" LeFleur said.

Dobby shook his head. "Strange name."

"Yeah."

Through the windshield, LeFleur saw the large sign that read "Now Leaving Volcano Hazard Zone." He felt a pang of relief. They were back on the island's north side. Back to the living.

"Another twenty minutes," he said.

"Can I get something to eat?" Dobby asked. "Before you lock me up?"

Two hours later, after dropping Dobby at the island's only jail, LeFleur returned to his office and flicked on the lights. He was bone-tired. He took the notebook from his briefcase and placed it in on his desk. Then he leaned his forehead into his hands, shut his eyes, and rubbed hard, as if to shake loose an answer from his brain.

Nothing came. He was back to where he'd begun. A sunken yacht. A discovered raft. An unbelievable story. An accused with an excuse.

He wanted a drink. He pulled open his lower drawer,

where he stashed small bottles of rum that he picked up at the island factory. Katrina, his assistant, would periodically throw those bottles away. A churchgoing woman, she didn't approve of him drinking on the job, but she wouldn't dare say that to him directly. So he'd get the little bottles and they'd be there for a while, then one day they'd be gone and he knew she had tossed them. He never confronted her. It was their little game.

This time, when he opened the lower drawer, something else caught his eye. A large tan envelope with the precinct's stamp on the upper left-hand corner. Except the envelope was sealed.

He dialed Katrina, who sounded surprised to hear from him.

"Where were you all day?" she asked. "People were asking for you."

"Yeah," he said, "I had to take care of something. Hey. Did you put a sealed envelope in my desk?"

"What?"

"In my drawer. You know. The *lower* drawer?"

"Oh, yeah. That was last week, from that guy. Remember? That day you were stuck in Marguerita Bay?"

"Rom?"

"I don't know his name. He never told me. He asked for an envelope while he was waiting, so I gave him one. You said it was OK, remember? And then, like I told you, when

I came back out to find him, he was gone. But he left the envelope on the steps, so I put it in your desk."

"Why didn't you tell me?"

"I did." She paused. "I *thought* I did. Oh, Jarty. There's so much going on. I'm sorry if I forg—"

But LeFleur had already hung up. He ripped open the envelope to find a stack of folded pages. The edges were frayed and the handwriting was familiar. LeFleur knew exactly where they had come from.

He started reading so fast he didn't even feel himself drop back into his chair.

Sea

~~~~~~

My Dear Annabelle.

One final time, I beg your forgiveness. It's been months since I wrote you anything. I am still at sea, but no longer at war with it. I may live. I may die. It doesn't matter. A shroud has been lifted. I can say all I need to say now.

I'd be quite a sight to you, my love. There is much less of me. My arms are scrawny. My thighs are thin chops. Some of my teeth are loose. The clothes I used to wear are just shreds of fabric, chewed away by the pervasive salt. The only thing there is more of is my beard, which is growing unfettered toward my collarbone.

I don't know how far across the Atlantic I have traveled. One night I saw a large boat on the horizon. I fired a flare. Nothing. Weeks later, I spotted a cargo ship, so close

I could make out the colors on her hull. Another flare. Nothing.

I have accepted that rescue will be impossible. I am too small. Too insignificant. I am a man in a raft, and if I am to survive, the currents hold my fate. The oceans of the world are all connected, Annabelle, so perhaps I am meant to pass from one to another in a ceaseless looping of the planet. Or maybe, in the end, Mother Sea will take me, as a mother bear takes her weak and sickly cub. Put me out of my misery. Perhaps that would be best.

Whatever awaits, that's what will be. The sick and elderly sometimes say, "Let me go. I am ready to meet the Lord." But what need do I have for such surrender? I have met the Lord already.

Looking back on these pages, I see I stopped writing after little Alice spoke for the first time.

I remember only darkness after that. I must have blacked out. The shock of losing Lambert and Geri, the effort of swimming after weeks of inactivity—all that left me a gasless tank.

When I came to, the sun was gone and the evening sky was an indigo blue. Alice was sitting on the edge of the raft, lit by moonlight, her narrow arms crossed in her lap.

She wore one of Geri's white T-shirts, which hung over her knees. The bangs of her hair fluttered with the breeze.

"Alice?" I whispered.

"Why do you call me that?" she said.

Her voice was childlike, yet clear and precise.

"We had to call you something," I said. "What's your real name?"

She smiled. "Alice will do."

My throat was dry, and my eyes were sticky with sleep. As I turned my head, the empty raft brought a sickening wave of grief.

"Everyone is *gone*."

"Yes," she said.

"The sharks got Geri. I couldn't save her. And Lambert. I couldn't save him, either."

I thought about those final moments in the water. Then I remembered.

"Alice?" I said, lifting to my elbows. "Did you say you were . . . *the Lord*?"

"I am."

"What do you mean?"

"Just what I said."

"But you're a *child*."

"Isn't the Lord in all children?"

I blinked several times. My thinking was foggy.

"Wait . . . then who was the man we pulled from the water?"

She didn't answer.

"Alice?" My voice rose. "Why did that man die? Are you just mimicking him? Who are you really? Why didn't you speak before now?"

She uncrossed her arms, got to her feet, and walked toward me without the slightest wobble. She crouched by my side, and crossed her small legs in front of her. I stared, wordless, as she lifted my right hand and placed it inside hers.

"Sit with me, Benjamin," she said.

And we sat. Through the evening—and through the night—without saying another word. It's not that I couldn't speak, Annabelle. It's that the inclination was suddenly gone. I know it sounds strange, but all protest within me had vanished. Holding her hand was like a key turning a tumbler. My body melted. My breath calmed. As the minutes passed, I seemed to get smaller. The heavens grew enormous. When a spread of glowing stars took over the sky, it drew tears from my eyes.

We sat like that until the dawn, when the sun broke over the horizon and its rays shot out in every direction. The reflection sent a path of glimmering diamonds through the chop and all the way to our raft. In that moment, it was possible to believe that the world was nothing more than water and sky, that land was not even a concept, and all that man had built upon it was inconsequential. I realized this is what it means to forgo everything and be alone with God.

And I knew that I was.

"Now, Benjamin," Alice said softly, "ask me what you wish."

My voice felt buried deep in my windpipe. I dragged the words up like a bucket from a well.

"Who was he? The man who called himself the Lord?"

"An angel I spoke through."

"Why did he ask for food and water?"

"To see if you would share it."

"Why was he so quiet?"

"To see if you would listen."

I looked away. "Lambert killed him."

"Did he?" she said.

I turned back. Her expression was calm. I swallowed hard, unsure if I wanted to ask the next question, but knowing that I had to.

"Was Jason Lambert my father?"

She shook her head no.

I was instantly overwhelmed with emotion. The hate I had held for that man, the anger I had harbored toward the world because of him, it all came gushing out of me as if I were being socked continuously in the stomach. How wrong I was! How misdirected my rage! I banged my fists into the wet raft floor and howled until I reached the bottom of my soul. And there lay the question that has been driving my life every minute since I lost you.

I looked straight at Alice, and I asked it.

"Why did my wife have to die?"

She nodded as if this were expected. She placed her other hand on top of my palm.

"When someone passes, Benjamin, people always ask, 'Why did God take them?' A better question would be 'Why did God give them to us?' What did we do to deserve their love, their joy, the sweet moments we shared? Didn't you have such moments with Annabelle?"

"Every day," I rasped.

"Those moments are a gift. But their end is not a punishment. I am never cruel, Benjamin. I know you before you are born. I know you after you die. My plans for you are not defined by this world.

"Beginnings and endings are earthly ideas. I go on. And because I go on, you go on with me. Feeling loss is part of why you are on Earth. Through it, you appreciate the brief gift of human existence, and you learn to cherish the world I created for you. But the human form is not permanent. It was never meant to be. That gift belongs to the soul.

"I know the tears you shed, Benjamin. When people leave this Earth, their loved ones always weep." She smiled. "But I promise you, those who leave do not."

She lifted a hand and motioned upward. And at that instant, Annabelle, I can hardly describe it; the open air seemed to sweep aside, and the blue reflection of the atmosphere melted into the most brilliant light, a color for which I have no word. In that light, I saw more souls than there are stars in the sky. Yet somehow I could see the contented faces of each and every one of them. Among those faces, I saw my loving mother.

And I saw you.

I need nothing else.

Land

There were more pages, but LeFleur stopped reading. He stuffed them into his briefcase and wiped his eyes as he raced from the office.

He drove home trembling. He entered the yellow house and ran up the stairs. He put his hand on the door-knob of his daughter's room, and for the first time in four years, he turned it open. As he stood there, staring at the small bed and the pink stars he'd painted on the ceiling, Patrice stepped up behind him and said, "Jarty? What's going on?"

He turned and grabbed her close. Through heaving breath, he whispered, "Lilly's all right. She's all right. She's safe." And Patrice began crying, too.

"I know, sweetheart. I know she is."

They hugged each other tightly and later would not re-member how long they held that embrace. But they slept that night without waking up once. And when LeFleur opened his eyes the next morning, he felt something he had not felt in a very long time. He felt peace.

News

ANCHOR: *Tonight, an astonishing development in the search for the* Galaxy. *Our Tyler Brewer is aboard the exploration vessel the* Iliad.

REPORTER: *That's right, Jim. A discovery has been made. On the far end of the five-mile "search box," researchers spotted a large wreck on the ocean floor, about three miles down. It appears to be lying on its side. Ali Nesser of Nesser Ocean Explorations is with us here in what's called the "offline room" on the ship. Mr. Nesser, what are you seeing?*

ALI NESSER: *Late last night, our sonar system detected a large mass on the seabed. The data suggested a vessel approximately the size of the* Galaxy, *which gave us a strong suspicion that we'd located it. We then sent the Remotely Operated Vehicle or ROV down to take pictures of the wreckage. We received those images here on the screens behind me, and we're analyzing the data.*

REPORTER: *What does the data suggest?*

ALI NESSER: *Well, it's pitch-black down there, so everything we're getting is from the lights of our ROV. Still, we're confident this is the* Galaxy. *You can see the markings. And that was a pretty unique vessel.*

REPORTER: *Can you determine what caused her to sink?*

ALI NESSER: *No one should speculate on that until we have more data. But these images tell you a lot. Look at the hull. It's light fiberglass, which makes it susceptible to damage.*

REPORTER: *And by damage, you mean the hole we see?*

ALI NESSER: *That's just the bow. Look at this shot from the stern, where the engine room was located.*

REPORTER: *Those holes are even bigger.*

ALI NESSER: *That's right. Whatever happened, happened more than once. It wasn't one hole. It was three.*

Thirteen

Sea

~~~~~~

These will be the last words I write, my love. I realize now that you are always with me. I can share my thoughts just by picturing you. But on the chance that someone else finds this notebook, I want them to know the end of my story, and perhaps decide if it means anything at all.

The day after Alice opened the heavens for my view, it rained, and we were able to collect fresh water, enough to energize me into taking on tasks I'd felt too depressed or overwhelmed to try. I studied the broken solar still, and used some raft patch repair to plug up the hole. With the hot sun burning on the plastic, the condensation formed and eventually fresh drinking water collected in the reservoir. I also used the fishing line from the ditch kit and fashioned a hook from one of Mrs. Laghari's earrings that I'd had in my pants pocket that final night on the *Galaxy*.

I attached it with a knot, gripped the paddle-like handle, cast the line over the side, and waited for hours. Nothing. But the next morning, early, I tried again, and this time was able to snag a small sunfish. I ate most of it, saved a little meat for bait, and with that bait was able to catch a dorado the next day, which I cut into pieces and cured on lines I strung from one end of the canopy to the other. It was primitive fishing, but the newfound sustenance gave me a sharper focus. I felt my brain reviving.

Since then, I have been able to build a small stock of fish and potable water. My greatest foe has been loneliness, but with Alice alongside, I held that at bay. We spoke about many things. Yet deep down, I knew I was withholding the truth of my role in the *Galaxy*'s demise, just as I have been withholding it from you. I know it makes no sense, lying to the dead, or to the Lord. But we do it anyhow. Perhaps we hope that wherever they are, they will forgive us our shameful acts. No matter. In time, the truth comes out. Grief leads to anger, anger to guilt, guilt to confession.

Finally, one morning, I awoke to find the ocean as calm as a puddle. I blinked my eyes against the sun. Alice was standing over me.

"Go in the water," she said.

"Why?"

"It is time."

I didn't understand. Despite that, I felt myself rising.

"Take this with you," she said.

I glanced down. My eyes sprang open. Somehow, there, in the middle of the raft, was the green limpet mine. It looked the same as when I purchased it from a man I found on the Internet. I met him in a boat warehouse. Our transaction took less than ten minutes. I hid it in a drum case that I carried onto the *Galaxy*.

"Pick it up," Alice said. "And don't let it go."

I wanted to refuse, but my body did not operate on its own. I lifted that mine, felt its metal edges against my bare skin, and did as I was told.

When I hit the water, its cold enveloped me, and the weight of the mine sank me quickly. I dropped deeper and deeper. I closed my eyes, certain this was my penance. I was to die at the bottom of the sea, like the others who died because of me. All you do comes back to you. God's circular judgment.

As the water grew darker, I felt my body crying out to breathe, to expel the carbon dioxide accumulating in my blood. In a few seconds, my human form would submit. Water would fill my lungs, my brain would lose oxygen, and my death would come.

And yet, at that moment, Annabelle, I felt something new wash over me. Something liberating. After all that had happened, and everything I had done, I accepted this as a just ending, because I accepted the world as a just place. In that way, I accepted that God, or little Alice, or whatever force we all answer to, had justly determined my fate.

I believed. And in believing, I was saved.

Just as the Lord had promised.

Suddenly, my hands were empty. The mine was gone. Above me I saw a perfect circle of bright light, and in that circle was the entire sky and the sun, spraying rays like porcupine quills. My body began to drift up toward its center. I didn't have to do a thing. As I lifted, I felt certain that this is what it's like to die, and I saw there was nothing to fear from it. The Lord was right. A hovering Heaven is always waiting for us, visible from beneath the Earth's blue waters. Such a wondrous world.

⌒

Moments later I burst through the surface, gasping for breath. I saw the raft, maybe twenty yards away. I saw little Alice, waving her arms. "Here!" she yelled. "Over here!" And I realized I had heard that voice before, from someone with a flashlight the night the *Galaxy* sank.

When I reached the ladder, Alice helped me inside. I was gulping air as I tried to speak.

"It was you in the raft ... that night ... you saved me ..."

"Yes."

I fell to my knees and confessed everything. "I brought

the bomb onto the boat, Alice . . . It was me. Not Dobby. I planned to blow it up. It was my fault."

The words spilled out easier than I imagined, like a loose tooth that after hours of painful clinging suddenly slips onto your tongue.

"I was angry. I thought Jason Lambert was my father. I thought he'd done unforgivable things to my mother—and to me. I wanted him to suffer.

"I'd lost my wife, the only person who mattered to me. I couldn't afford her medical treatments. They cost too much money, money I never had but others did. I blamed myself. Everything seemed so unfair. I wanted revenge for all the suffering I'd gone through. I wanted Jason Lambert to lose as much as I did."

"His life," Alice said.

"Yes."

"It was not yours to take."

"I know that now," I said, looking down. "But . . ." I hesitated. "That's why I *never went through with it*. I never detonated that mine. I hid it away. Please believe me. Someone else must have exploded it. I can't explain. It's been torturing me ever since it happened. I'm sorry. I'm so sorry. I know I'm to blame . . ."

I began to cry. Alice touched my head softly, then rose to her feet.

"Do you remember the last thing you did on the *Galaxy* that night?" she asked.

I closed my eyes. I pictured myself in those final seconds on deck. The rain was beating down, my elbows were on the railing, my head was hanging low, staring at the dark waves. It was a terrible moment. I was thinking about how I had failed you, Annabelle, and the horror I'd been ready to commit in my grief, and what a pathetic, empty man I had become.

"Benjamin?" Alice asked again. "What was the last thing you did?"

My eyes opened slowly, as if coming out of a trance. Finally, with tears streaming down my cheeks, I confessed the truth, whispering the words I had been hiding all this time, from you, from Alice, from myself.

"I jumped."

⁓

A long time seemed to pass before I spoke again. Alice had her hands clasped under her chin.

"I didn't want to live anymore," I whispered.

"I know. I heard you."

"How? I never spoke."

"Despair has its own voice. It is a prayer unlike any other."

I looked down, ashamed of myself. "It doesn't matter.

The *Galaxy* blew up anyhow. I saw smoke from her engine room. I saw her go under. I didn't do it. But it's still my fault."

Alice walked to the rear of the raft. She stepped onto the tubed edge without the slightest hesitation. Then she turned back to me.

"Lift your head, Benjamin. You were not responsible."

I slowly raised my eyes.

"Wait . . . What do you mean?"

"The mine did not explode."

"I don't understand. Then what destroyed the ship?"

She turned her gaze out toward the deep. Suddenly, three massive whales burst through the surface, enormous charcoal monolithic bodies with flippers spread out like wings of a plane, easily the largest creatures I have ever witnessed on this Earth. When they hit the water, the spray from their impact flew through the air and covered us in seawater.

"They did," she said.

Moments later, the sky began to glow. The air went flat. I somehow sensed our time was over.

"Alice." I hesitated. "What do I do now?"

"Forgive yourself," she said. "Then use this grace to spread my spirit."

"How do I do that?"

"Survive this voyage. And once you do, find another soul in despair. And help them."

She spun on the raft edge, never lifting her small feet. Then she crossed her arms in front of her.

"Wait," I choked. "Don't leave me."

She smiled as if I'd said something funny. "I can never leave you."

With that, I collapsed, and my hands hit the wet raft floor. I was, at that moment, in complete submission. Alice looked at me one last time and recited the words that you, Annabelle, had spoken so often.

"We all need to hold on to something, Benji," she said. "Hold on to me."

She fell from the raft without a splash. I scrambled to the edge. I saw nothing but blue water.

News

ANCHOR: *We begin tonight with some startling findings in the strange saga of the* Galaxy *yacht, which sank more than a year ago. Here is Tyler Brewer from the island nation of Cape Verde.*

REPORTER: *Thank you, Jim. Last week, the robot probe from the* Iliad *returned to the* Galaxy *wreckage, this time releasing an even smaller robot camera about the size of a toaster. That device was able to enter the sunken yacht through its shattered hull and send back sharp images from the inside.*

ANCHOR: *And those findings were released today?*

REPORTER: *Yes. Preliminary reports claim that "repeated impacts to the yacht's exterior" created three sizable holes, and one of those impacted the engine room, which likely led to flooding and caused an explosion that quickened the sinking of the vessel. It was not believed to be a missile, as the holes in the hull do not conform to that sort of strike. One scientist postulated that whales, perhaps agitated by the loud music being played on board, could have been at fault, as whales are known to occasionally attack ships for such reasons. The bottom of the yacht was also painted red, a color that can attract those massive creatures.*

ANCHOR: *What about the passengers—or, to use the nautical language, the "souls" on the ship? What can you tell us?*

REPORTER: *Well, as you may recall, Jim, our own footage from that night showed that, due to a rainstorm, most of the guests were inside a small ballroom on the second level, listening to the band Fashion X, when the explosion occurred. Apparently, based on images from the probe, many of them died in that ballroom, and their remains can be seen and counted. Of course the* Galaxy's *actual manifests were all lost, and helicopters taking passengers back and forth make a definitive calculation impossible. But a Sextant spokesperson did tell us, "The number of identified remains is close to all the people we believe were on board."*

ANCHOR: *So it's unlikely anyone escaped or survived?*

REPORTER: *It appears that way.*

Epilogue

Land

LeFleur and Dobby sat inside the jeep, which was parked outside the small terminal of Montserrat's airport. A blue-and-white prop jet was landing on the single runway.

"I guess that's it," Dobby said, reaching for the door handle.

"Wait," LeFleur said. "I think you should have this."

He popped open the glove compartment and took out the plastic bag. It contained the original notebook, with the added pages folded inside it. He handed it to Dobby.

"You're sure?" Dobby said.

"He was your family."

Dobby examined the bag. He narrowed his gaze. "This can't get me in trouble, can it?"

"It doesn't exist," LeFleur said. "Anyhow, you were never on the ship. And it wasn't a mine that sank it. Really, it was nobody's fault."

"An act of God, huh?"

"I guess."

Dobby scratched his head. "Benji was really messed up. But he was still like my brother. I miss him badly." He paused. "How do you think he died?"

"Hard to say," LeFleur replied. "A storm? Another shark attack? Maybe, in the end, he just gave up. It's hard to survive that long on your own."

Dobby opened the door. "You know, you never did take me to where you found that raft."

"It's just a beach," LeFleur said. "Not far from here. Marguerita Bay."

"Maybe next visit," Dobby joked.

"Yeah," LeFleur said. He studied Dobby's face, the crow's-feet by his eyes, the stringy hair, the pale complexion. He was dressed once again in his black jeans and boots, ready to return to his life.

"Listen, I apologize for what I put you through early on," LeFleur said. "I just thought . . . well, you know."

Dobby nodded slowly. "We're both mourning someone we lost, Inspector."

"Jarty."

"Jarty," Dobby repeated, smiling. He got out of the car, took a step, then turned back. "Speaking of names, I think it's Rum Rosh."

"What?"

"Rum Rosh. It's in Psalms, the original Hebrew. It means 'God lifted my head.' I learned it as a kid. A priest taught me. The Irish and their churches, you know."

LeFleur stared at him. "What are you saying?"

"I think whoever found that raft was having a laugh on you, Jarty."

He threw his duffel over his shoulder and walked into the terminal.

LeFleur drove back toward his office, thinking about what Dobby had said. He pictured the first day he and Rom had met, and their trip up to Marguerita Bay. Rom had let LeFleur examine the raft by himself. And every time LeFleur glanced over, Rom was looking away, staring at the hills, as if he'd never seen the place before.

But he *had* seen the place before. Otherwise how would he have reported the location? And Marguerita Bay was not easy to get to; you had to park on that lookout and walk down that path. Teenagers would often hang out there, smoking and drinking, because they could easily hide if they saw someone coming . . .

LeFleur hit the brakes and spun the jeep around.

⌒

Twenty minutes later, he was hurrying down that path to the water. When he reached the beach, he removed his shoes and splashed along the wet sand. The sky was without clouds, and the sea came up a turquoise blue. As he edged around a tall rock formation, he saw a thin, bearded figure sitting in the distance, leaning back on his palms, as small waves broke and reached his legs before retreating.

LeFleur got within a few feet before the man turned his head.

"Rom?"

"Hello, Inspector."

"A lot of folks have been looking for you."

The man said nothing. LeFleur squatted down next to him.

"How long have you been on this island? Really?"

"A little while."

"And that raft had been here long before you came to the station."

"That's right."

"You always knew I'd find that notebook, didn't you? You'd already read it."

"Yes."

"And you left me those last pages in that envelope."

"I did."

LeFleur pursed his lips. "Why?"

"I thought they might help you." Rom turned. "Did they?"

"Yeah," LeFleur sighed. "Actually, they did." He paused, studying Rom's face. "But how did you know I needed help?"

"When we first met. The photo of your family. Your wife. Your little girl. I saw the pain in your eyes. I knew you must have lost someone in that picture."

LeFleur grunted. Rom raked his hands through the sand.

"Did you believe the story you read, Inspector?"

"Some of it."

"Which part?"

"Well. I believe Benji was in the raft."

"Just him?"

LeFleur thought. "No. Not just him."

Rom wiggled his fingers and produced a tiny crab. He held it up. "Did you know a crab will escape its shell thirty times before it dies?" He looked out to sea. "This world can be a trying place, Inspector. Sometimes you have to shed who you were to live who you are."

"Is that why you changed your name?" LeFleur asked. "Rum Rosh? 'God lifted your head'?"

The man smiled but never looked his way. LeFleur felt the hot sun on the back of his neck. He stared at the empty blue horizon. The distance from Cape Verde to this beach was thousands of miles.

"How did you do it, Benji? How did you survive all that way alone?"

"I was never alone," the man said.

Over time, Montserrat quieted considerably. The journalists departed. The raft was shipped to a Boston laboratory. Leonard Sprague, the police commissioner, was disappointed that the media attention, while sparking curiosity, did not increase tourist travel to the island.

The TV reporter Tyler Brewer won an award for his extensive *Galaxy* coverage, then went on to other stories. The company that insured the yacht was forced to pay a large settlement after analysts concluded that the sinking was caused not by neglect but rather by a mammal attack that broke holes in the fragile hull and caused a catastrophic explosion in the engine room.

The families of those lost at sea felt a certain closure, knowing the final resting place of their loved ones. And in the weeks that followed, a few of those families received unusual correspondence. Alexander Campbell, the youngest son of Nevin Campbell, got an unsigned letter that stated his father's regrets at not spending more time with him. Dev Bhatt, the husband of Mrs. Latha Laghari, received an envelope with two earrings inside it.

Six months later, Jarty LeFleur and his wife Patrice went to a doctor and learned that Patrice was pregnant. "Are you serious?" she said, then broke into tears and grabbed her husband, whose mouth dropped open in happy astonishment.

And not long after that, a rent-a-car drove to the lookout above Marguerita Bay, and a man in black jeans and boots walked down to the beach, holding a tattered notebook. When he spotted a thin man heading his way, they both started running, yelling each other's names, until they embraced in a long-awaited reunion.

In the end, there is the sea and the land and the news that happens between them. To spread that news, we tell each other stories. Sometimes the stories are about survival. And sometimes those stories, like the presence of the Lord, are hard to believe. Unless believing is what makes them true.

Acknowledgements

First, I'd like to thank you, beloved readers, for making time for my stories. May the stranger in your lifeboat always guide you, inspire you, and shine upon you.

Next, although this is a work of fiction, I did rely upon some real-life help to make the ocean scenes as legitimate as possible. To that end, I would like to thank Jo-Ann Barnas for her excellent research, and through her efforts, appreciation to Mark Pillsbury, Editor, Cruising World; and A. J. Barnas, a marine operations manager.

Special thanks to (the real) Ali Nesser for his keen reading and shipwreck salvation expertise. In addition, although not directly involved with this book, I'd like to acknowledge the many inspirational people of faith who influenced my thinking on the subject, including Albert

Lewis, Henry Covington, David Wolpe, Steve Linderman, and Yonel Ismael.

I have a team of people who help me work and allow me the space to go off and create imaginary life rafts, and I wish to acknowledge and thank them for that blessing: Rosey, Mendel, Kerri, Vince, Rick, and Trish.

As always, thanks to my editor, the wonderful Karen Rinaldi, who sparked to this idea right away (long before she knew who the stranger was), and to my friend and longtime agent, David Black, who makes me feel that any book I am writing is a special one.

Equal appreciation to all those at Harper who support my work, including Jonathan Burnham, Doug Jones, Leah Wasielewski, Tom Hopke, Haley Swanson, Rebecca Holland, Viviana Moreno, and Leslie Cohen, who works very hard to let the world know about my books. And once again, Milan Bozic, for designing another in a series of memorable covers.

Thanks to all the good people at Black Inc, including Ayla Zuraw Friedland, Rachel Ludwig, and the inimitable Susan Raihoffer, who brings my stories to the world and returns to tell me what the world thinks of them.

Special thanks to Antonella Iannarino, who keeps me connected to the digital universe. And to Ashley Sandberg, who finds new ways to share my stories with audiences everywhere.

The earliest readers of this book were teenagers at the Have Faith Haiti Orphanage in Port-au-Prince, Haiti, and I thank them for their remarkable input. I marvel every day at their tireless faith.

And, since you are who you are thanks largely to your family, I wish to acknowledge my parents, Ira and Rhoda Albom, even though this, sadly, is my first novel neither one of them are here to read; my sister, Cara; my brother Peter; my many brothers and sisters-in-law; my beloved nieces, nephews, and cousins; and my parents-in-law, Tony and Maureen.

Finally, at the end of all your stories is the one you love, and at the end of mine is always Janine.

About the Author

Mitch Albom is an internationally renowned author, journalist, screenwriter, playwright, broadcaster, and musician. He is the author of seven number one *New York Times* bestsellers. His books have collectively sold more than forty million copies worldwide and have been published in forty-nine territories and in forty-seven languages. They have been made into Emmy Award–winning and critically acclaimed television movies. Albom oversees nine charities under his SAY Detroit umbrella. He also operates the Have Faith Haiti Orphanage in Port-au-Prince, Haiti, which he visits every month. He lives in Michigan with his wife, Janine.